COLLECT THE SET!

Boffin Boy and the Invaders from Space
978 184167 613 5

Boffin Boy and the Wizard of Edo
978 184167 614 2

Boffin Boy and the Monsters from the Deep
978 184167 615 9

Boffin Boy and the Red Wolf
978 184167 616 6

Boffin Boy and the Lost City
978 184167 617 3

Boffin Boy and the Time Warriors
978 184167 622 7

Boffin Boy and the Ice Caves of Pluto
978 184167 626 5

Boffin Boy and the Quest for Wisdom
978 184167 628 9

Boffin Boy and the Deadly Swarm
978 184167 625 8

Boffin Boy and the Rock Men
978 184167 624 1

Boffin Boy and the Temples of Mars
978 184167 623 4

Boffin Boy and the Forest of the Ninja
978 184167 627 2

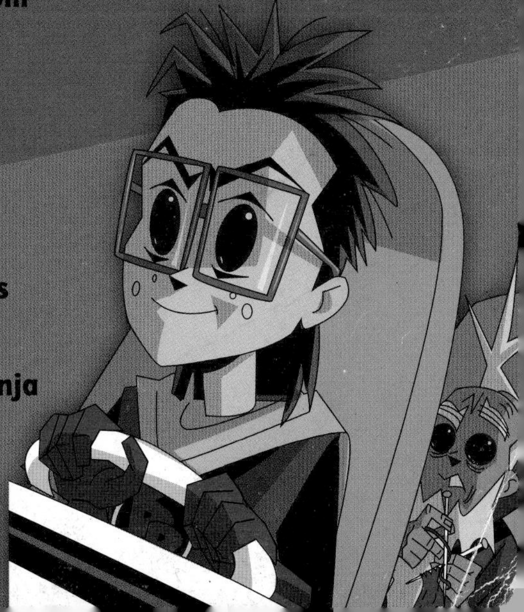

Boffin Boy and the Temples of Mars
by David Orme

Illustrated by Peter Richardson

Published by Ransom Publishing Ltd.
51 Southgate Street, Winchester, Hants. SO23 9EH
www.ransom.co.uk

ISBN   978 184167 623 4
First published in 2007
Reprinted 2008, 2009
A CIP catalogue record of this book is available from the British Library.
Design & layout: *www.macwiz.co.uk*

Find out more about Boffin Boy at *www.ransom.co.uk*.

Boffin Boy and the Temples of Mars

By David Orme

Illustrated by Peter Richardson

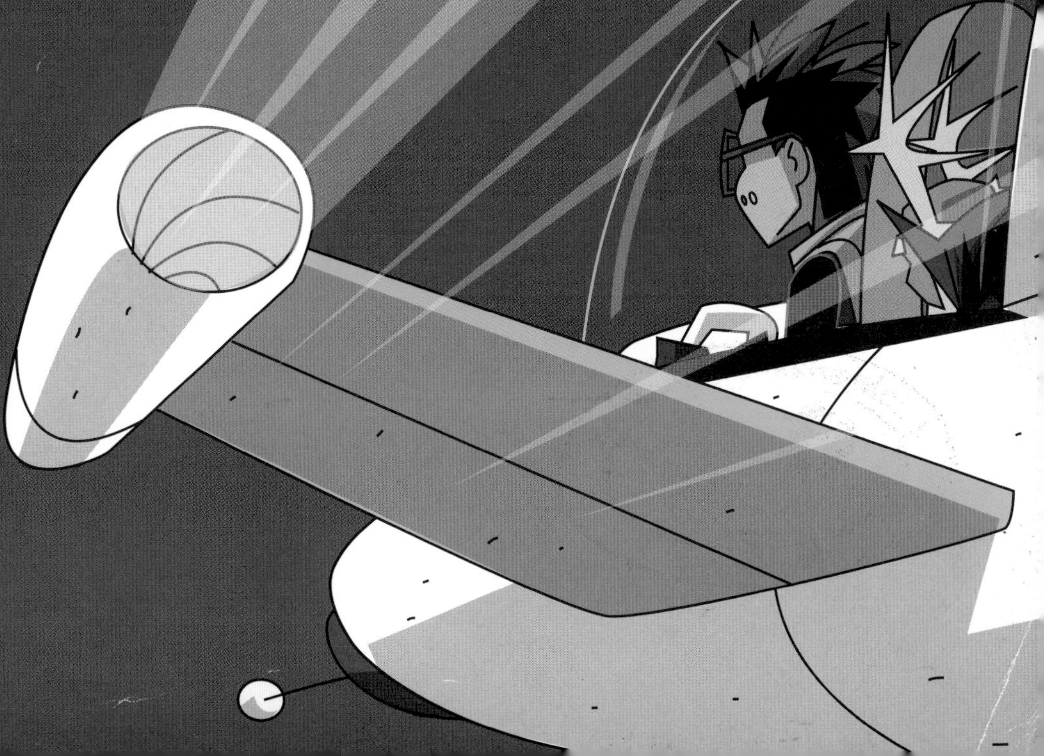

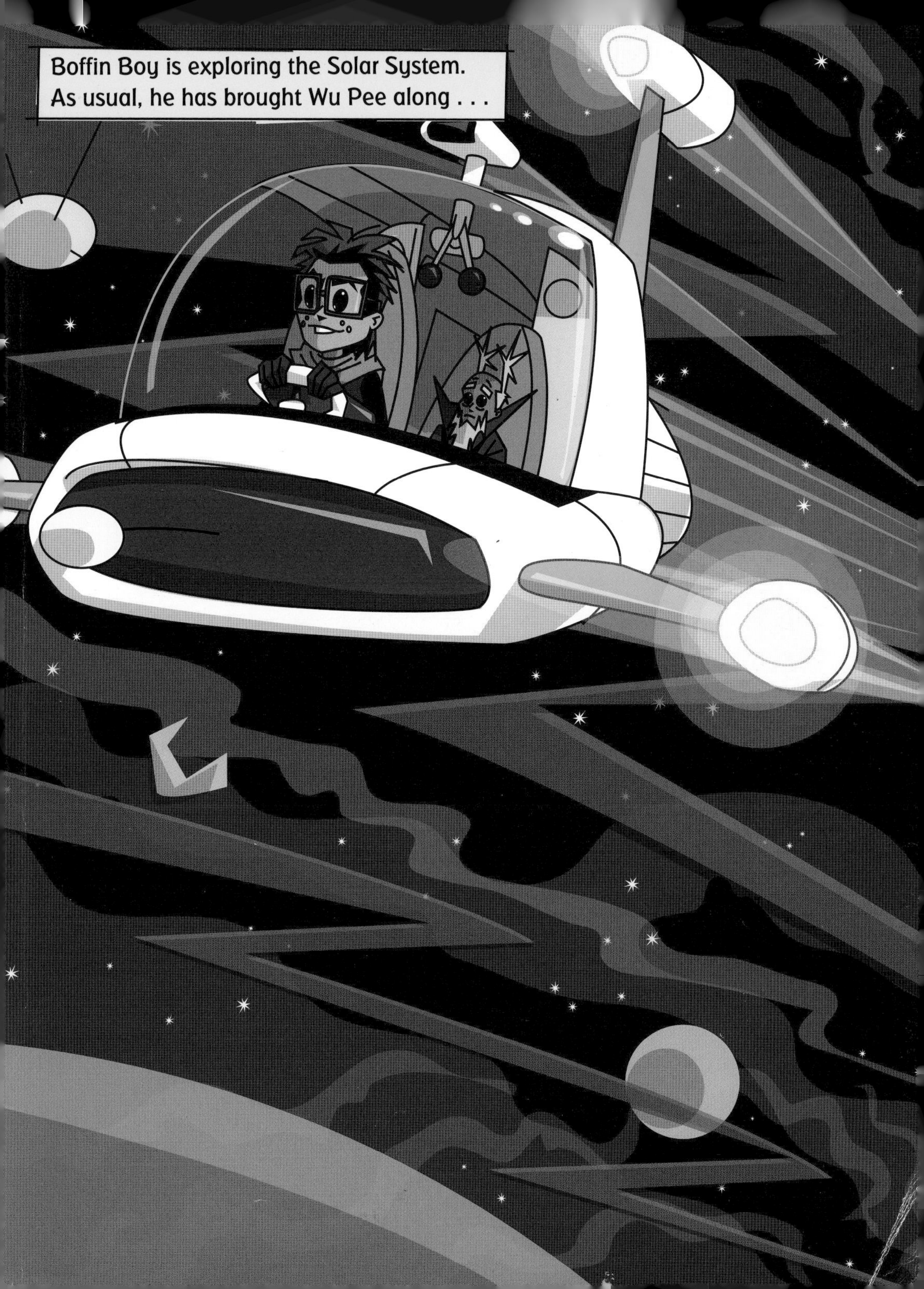
Boffin Boy is exploring the Solar System.
As usual, he has brought Wu Pee along . . .

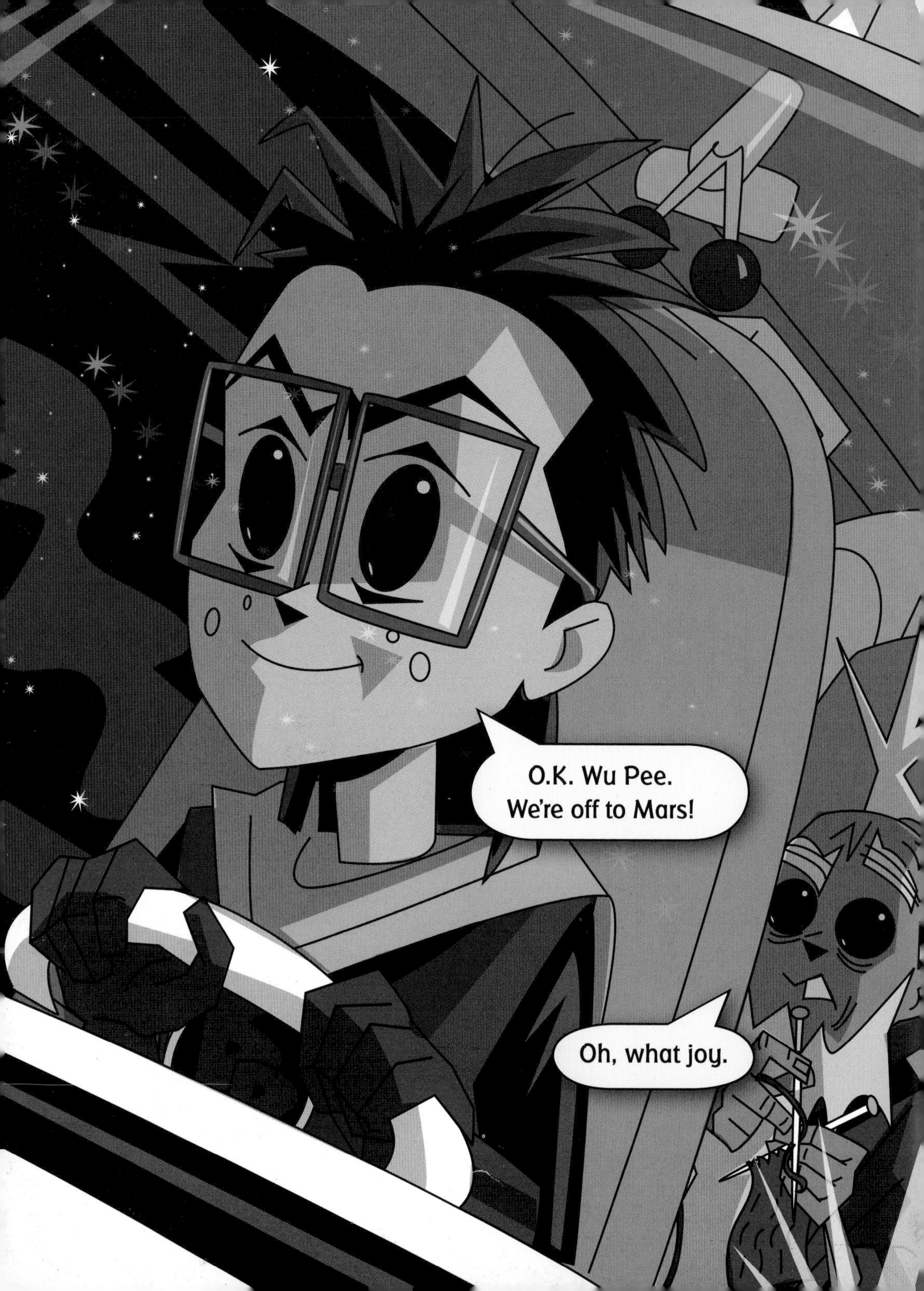
O.K. Wu Pee.
We're off to Mars!
Oh, what joy.

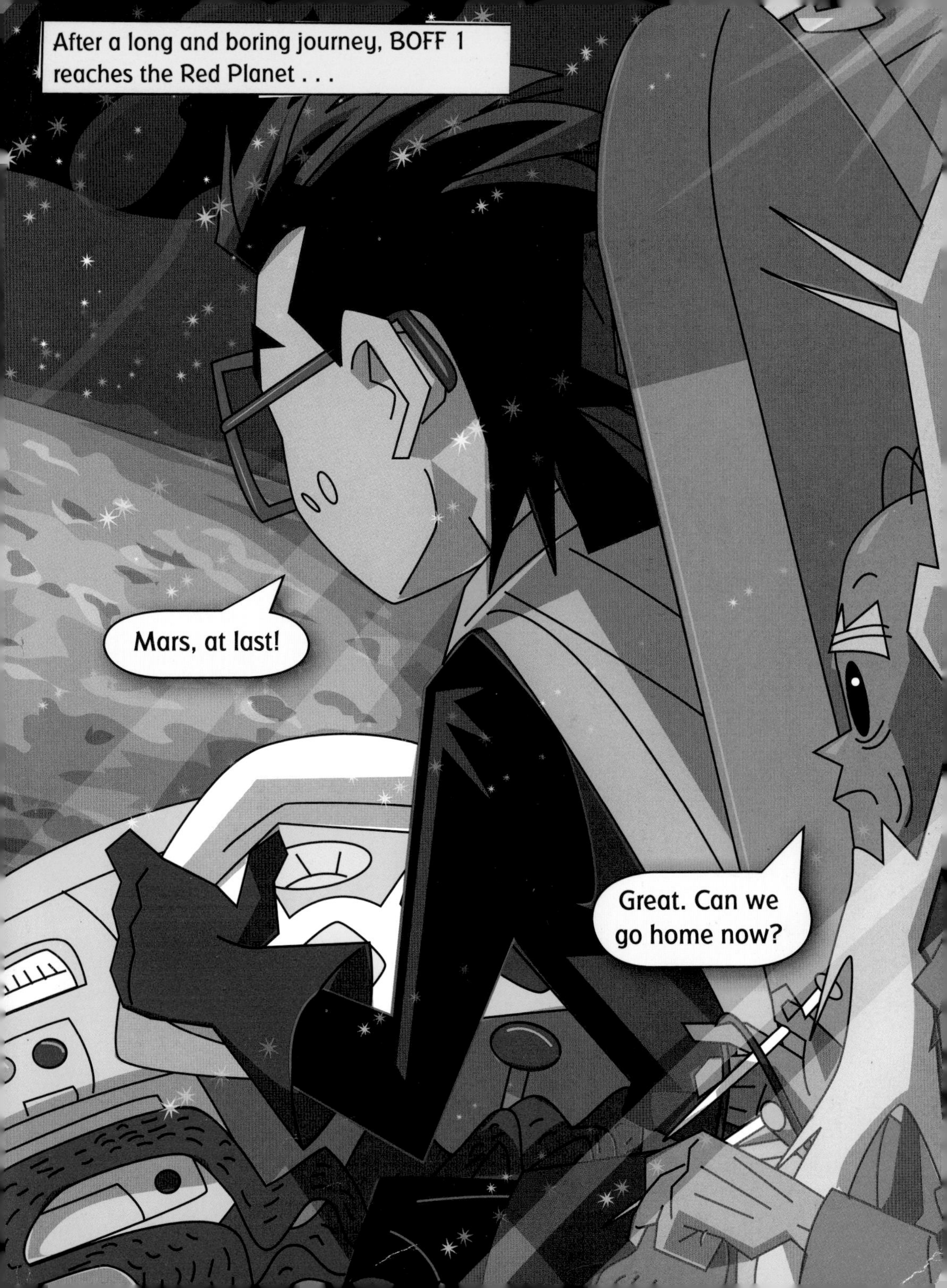
After a long and boring journey, BOFF 1 reaches the Red Planet . . .
Mars, at last!
Great. Can we go home now?

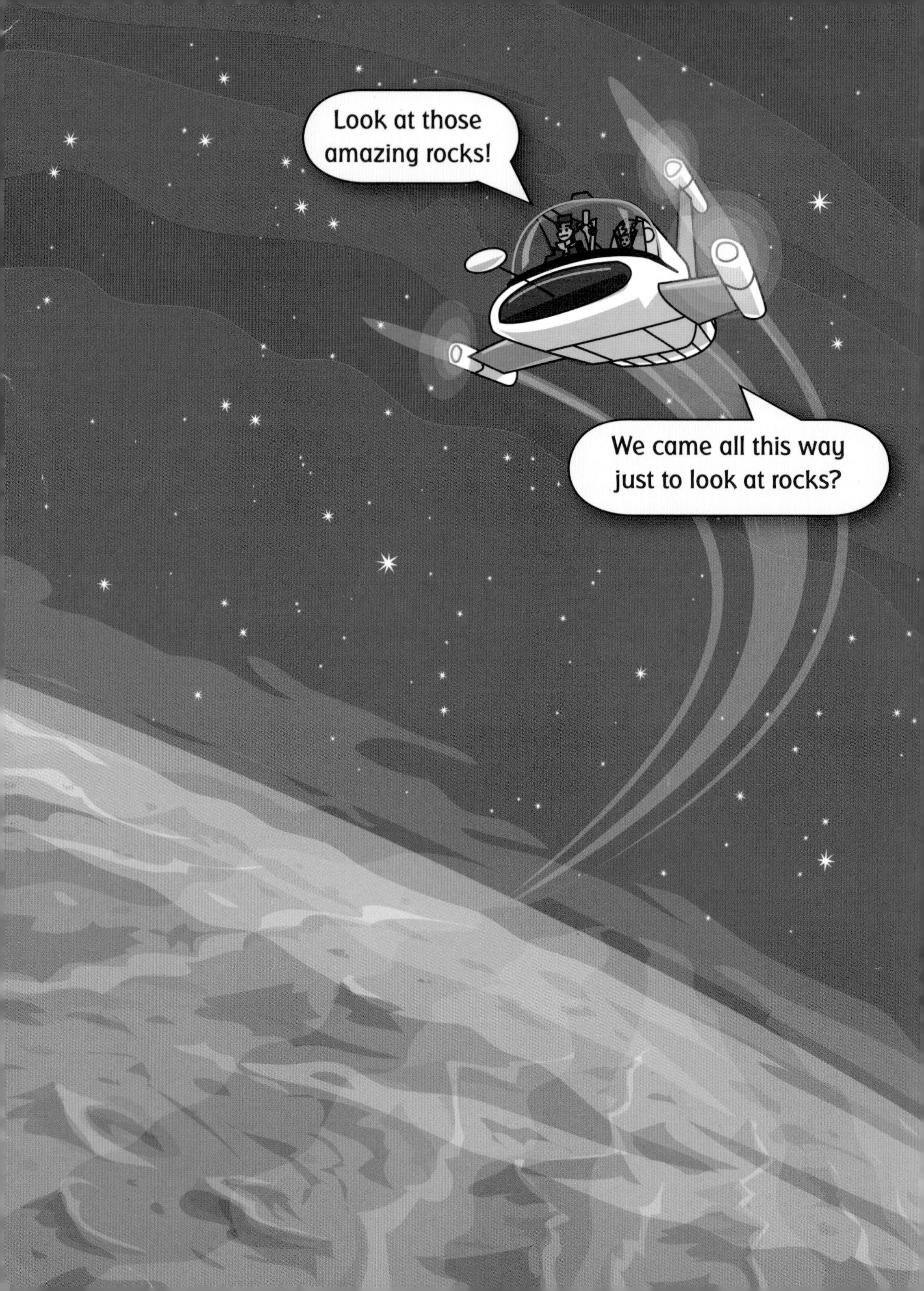
Look at those amazing rocks!
We came all this way just to look at rocks?

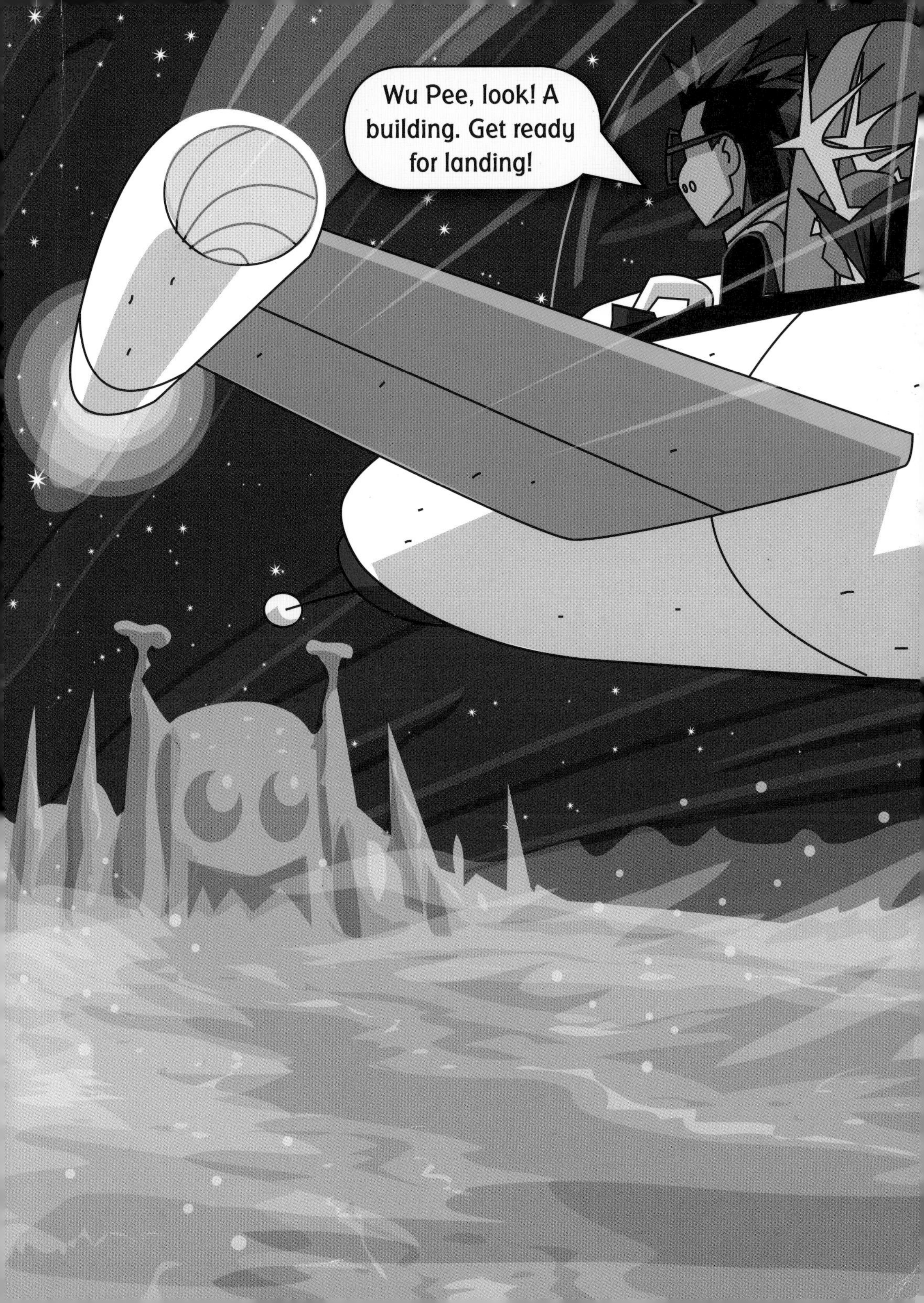
Wu Pee, look! A building. Get ready for landing!

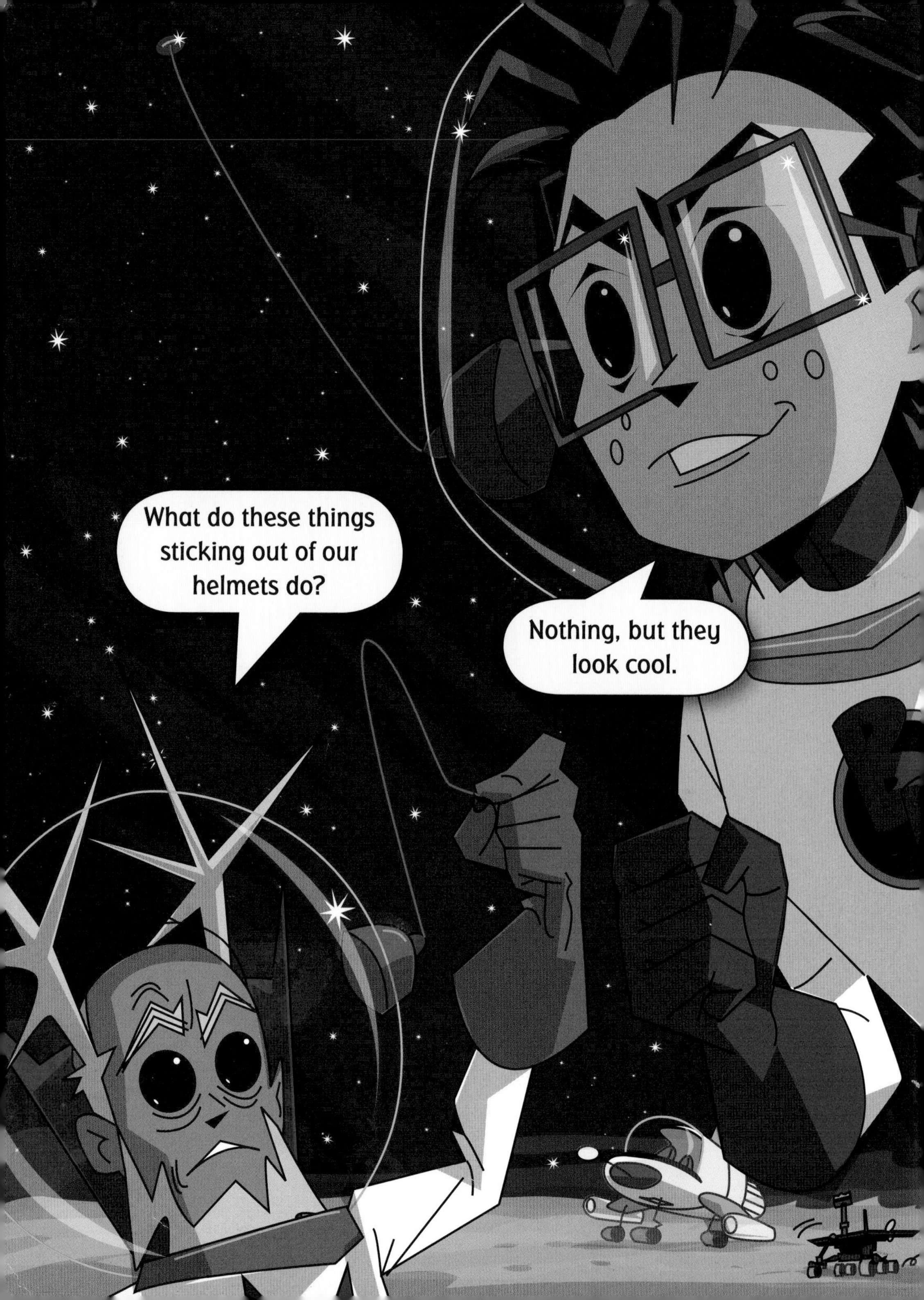
What do these things sticking out of our helmets do?
Nothing, but they look cool.

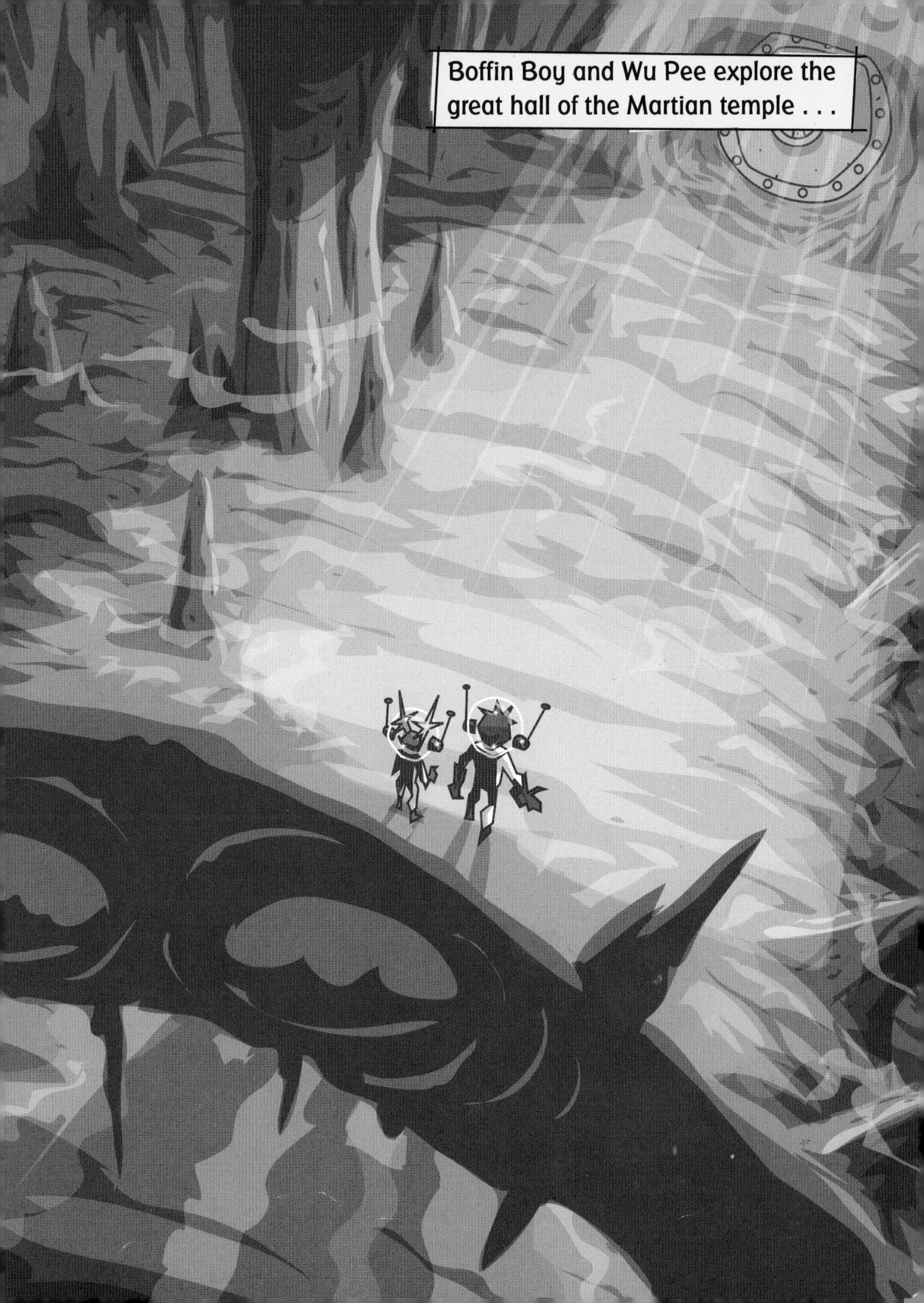
Boffin Boy and Wu Pee explore the great hall of the Martian temple . . .

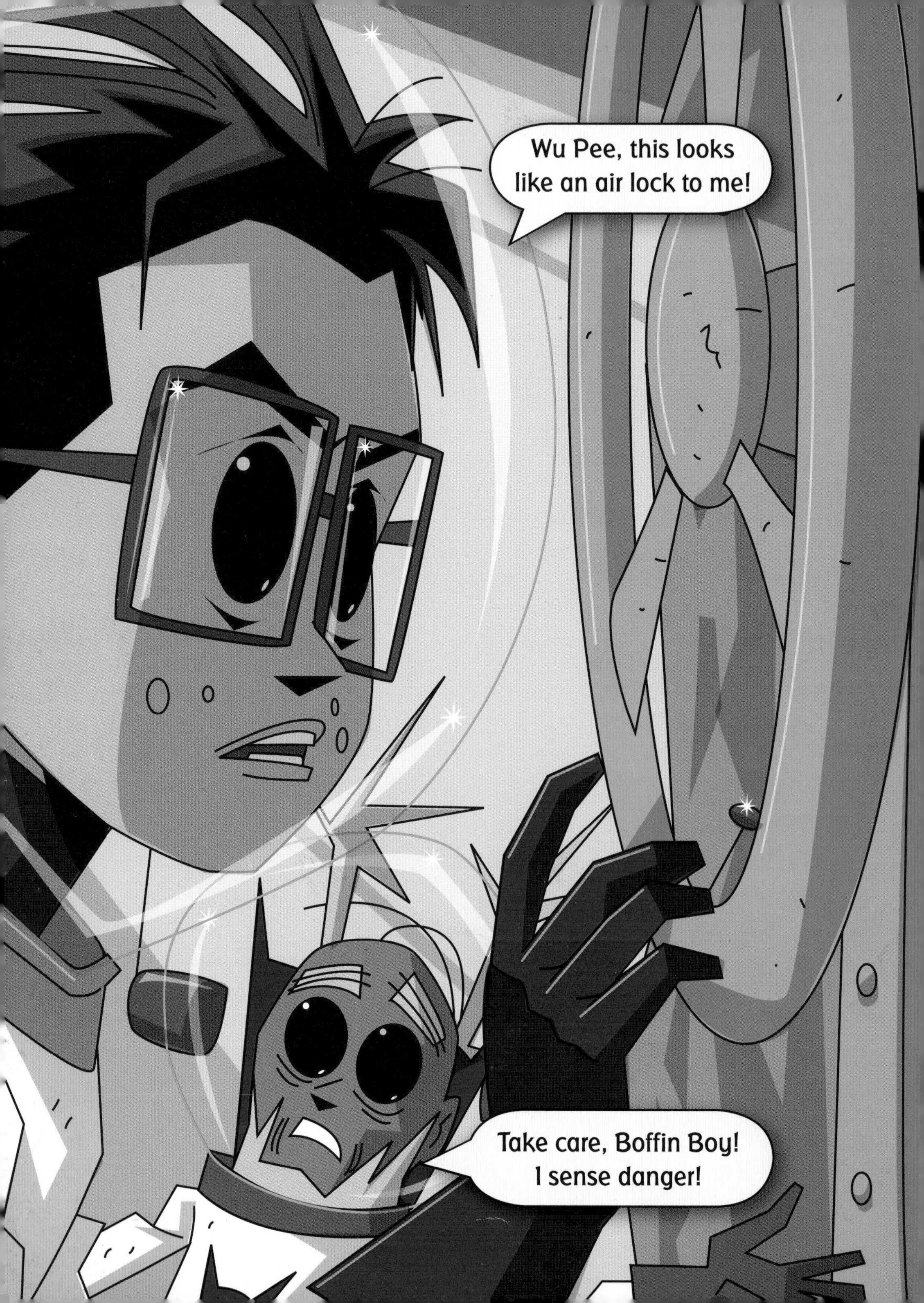
Wu Pee, this looks like an air lock to me!
Take care, Boffin Boy! I sense danger!

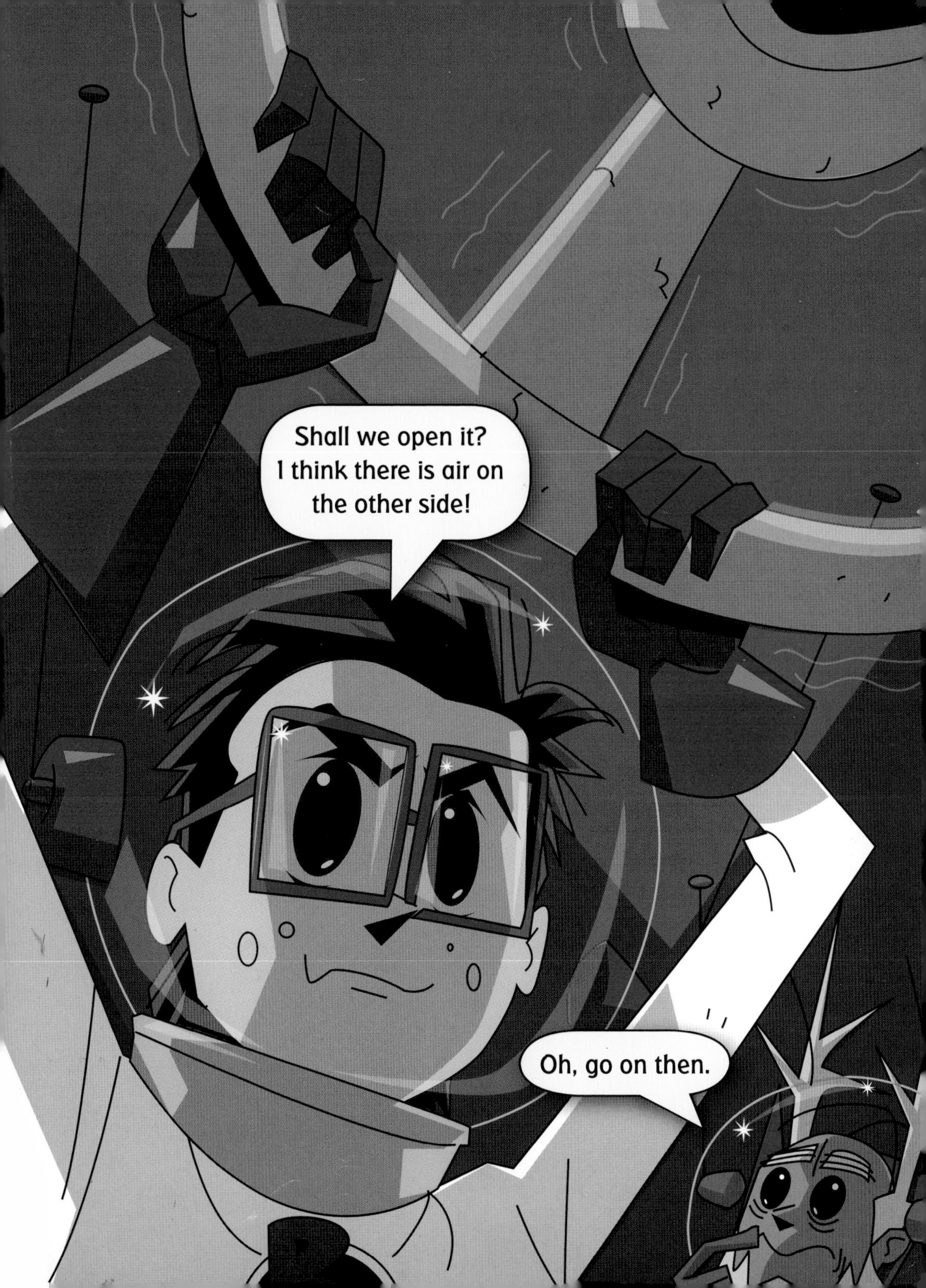
Shall we open it? I think there is air on the other side!
Oh, go on then.

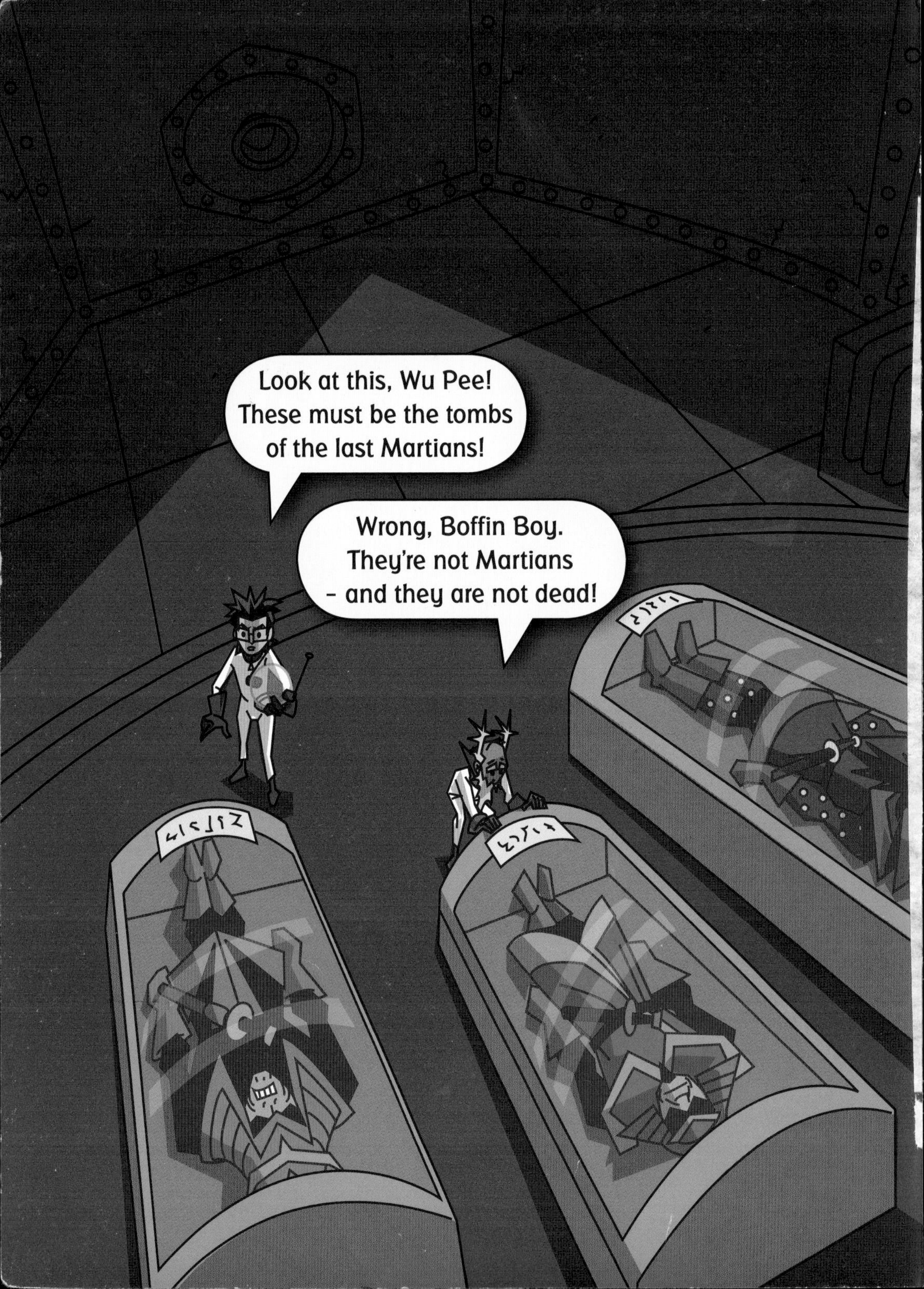
Look at this, Wu Pee! These must be the tombs of the last Martians!
Wrong, Boffin Boy. They're not Martians – and they are not dead!

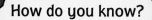

How do you know?

I can read these words!
These are wise men from Earth,
Boffin Boy. They must have
invented space travel thousands of
years before our own age.
It says here, 'Do not wake us
unless the Earth is in danger!'

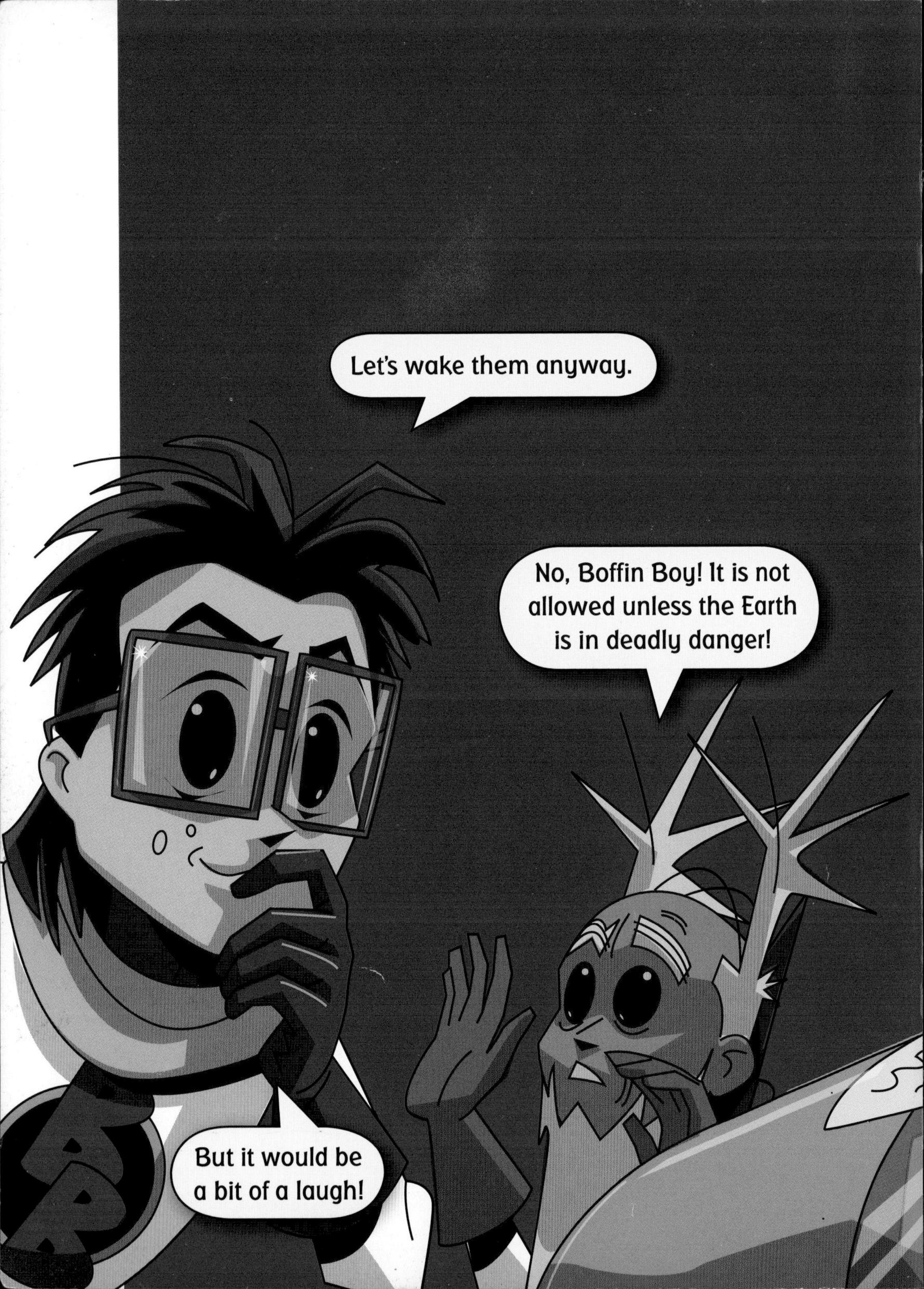
Let's wake them anyway.
No, Boffin Boy! It is not allowed unless the Earth is in deadly danger!
But it would be a bit of a laugh!

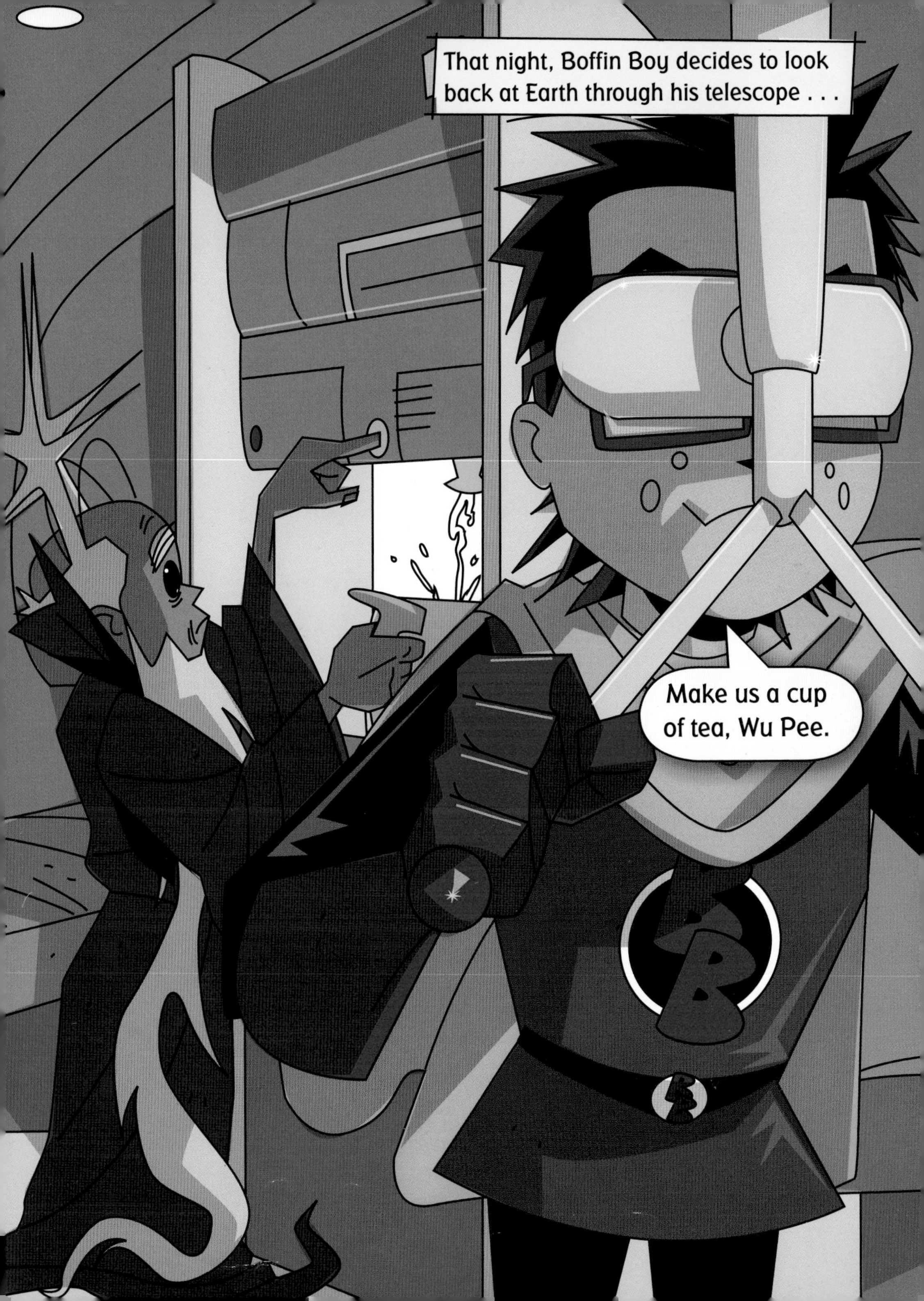
That night, Boffin Boy decides to look back at Earth through his telescope . . .
Make us a cup of tea, Wu Pee.

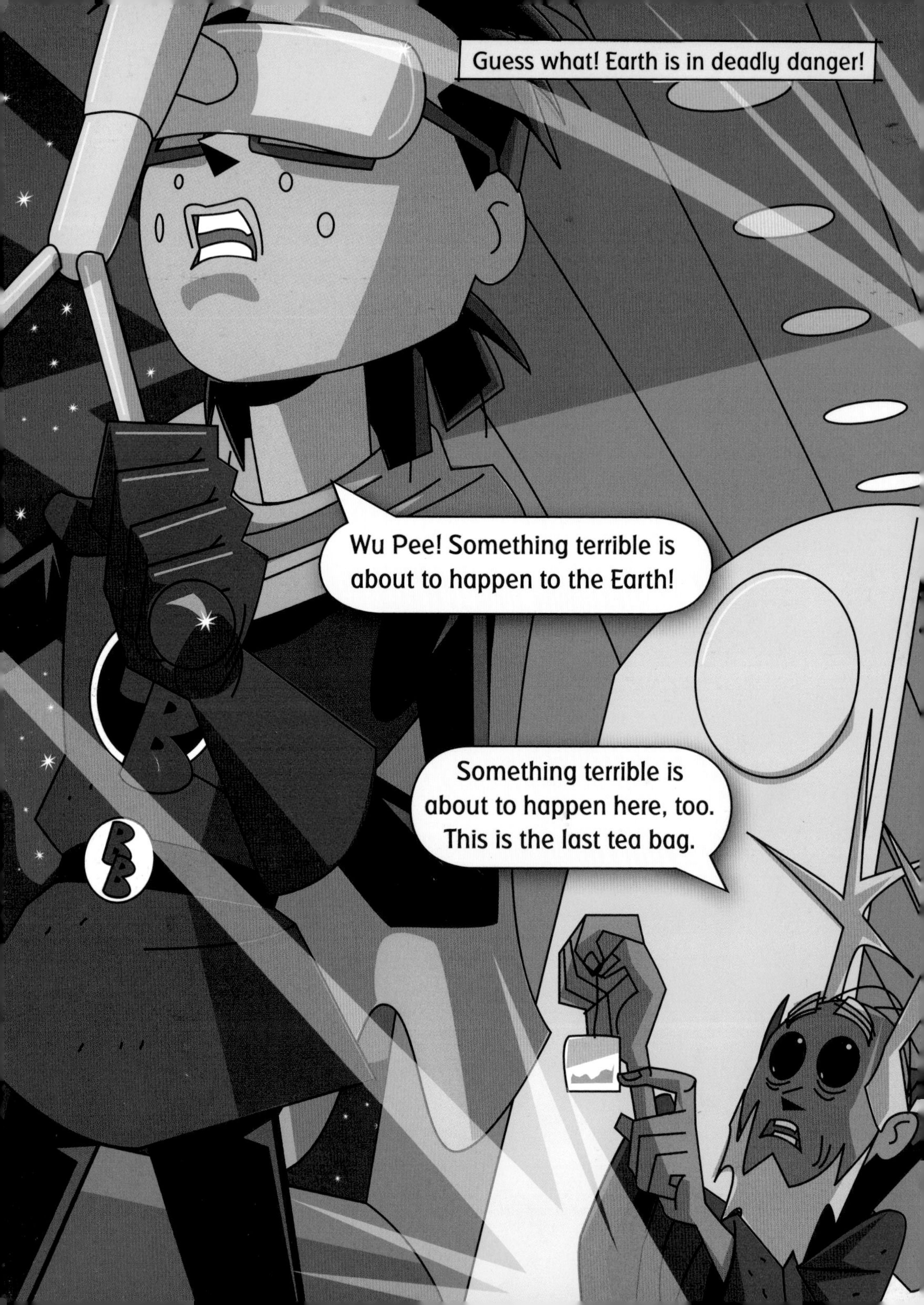
Guess what! Earth is in deadly danger!
Wu Pee! Something terrible is about to happen to the Earth!
Something terrible is about to happen here, too. This is the last tea bag.

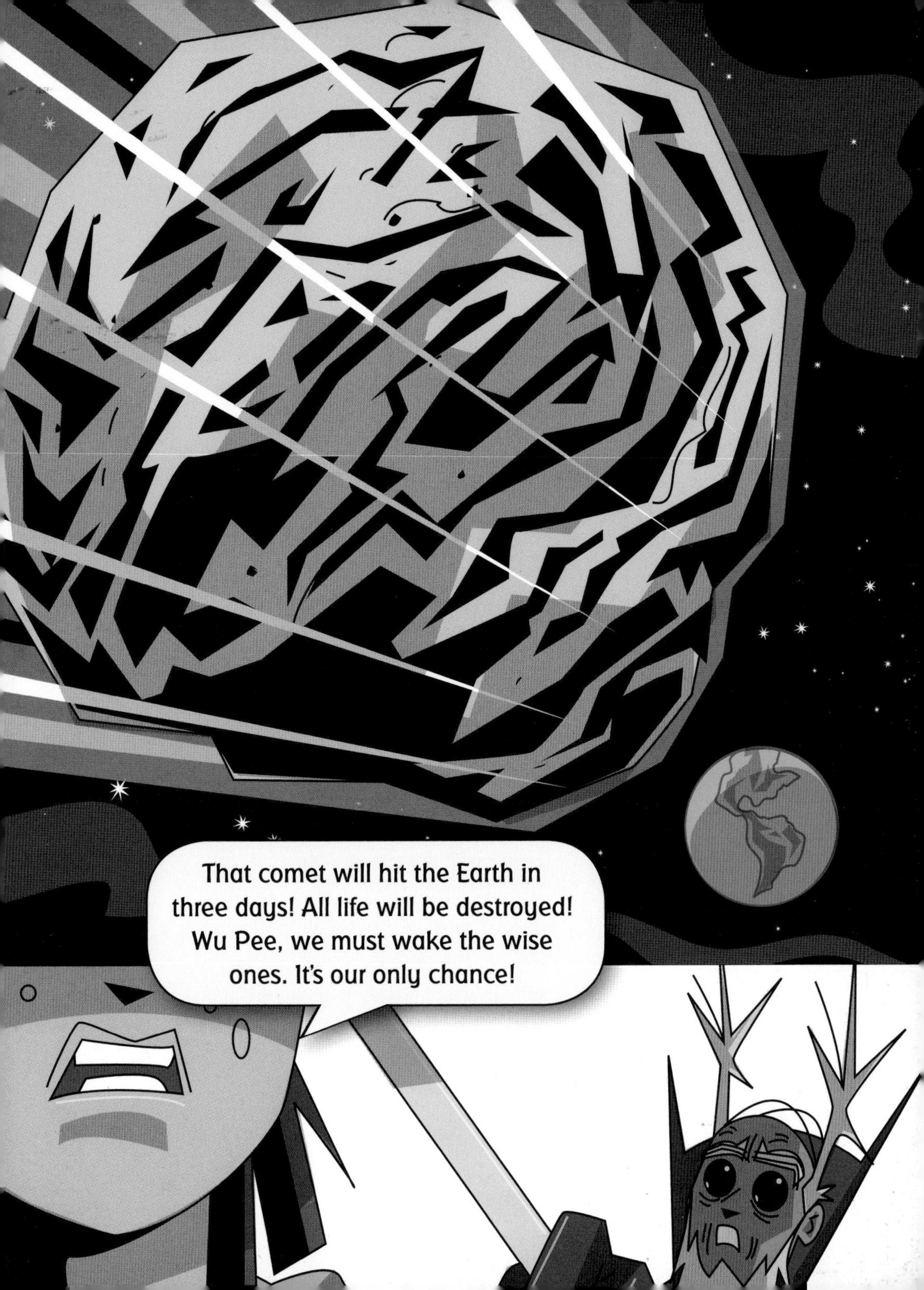
That comet will hit the Earth in three days! All life will be destroyed! Wu Pee, we must wake the wise ones. It's our only chance!

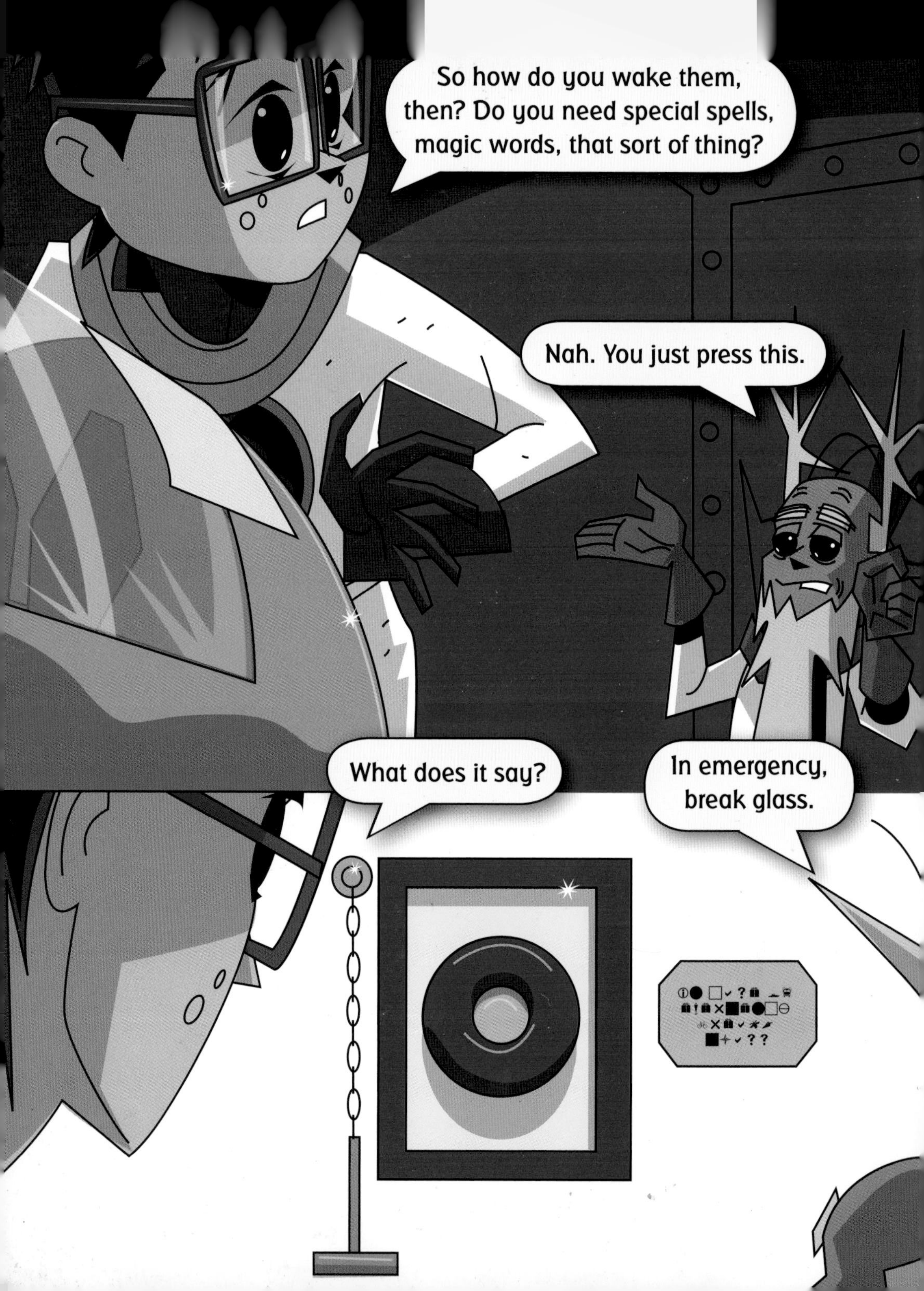
So how do you wake them, then? Do you need special spells, magic words, that sort of thing?
Nah. You just press this.
What does it say?
In emergency, break glass.

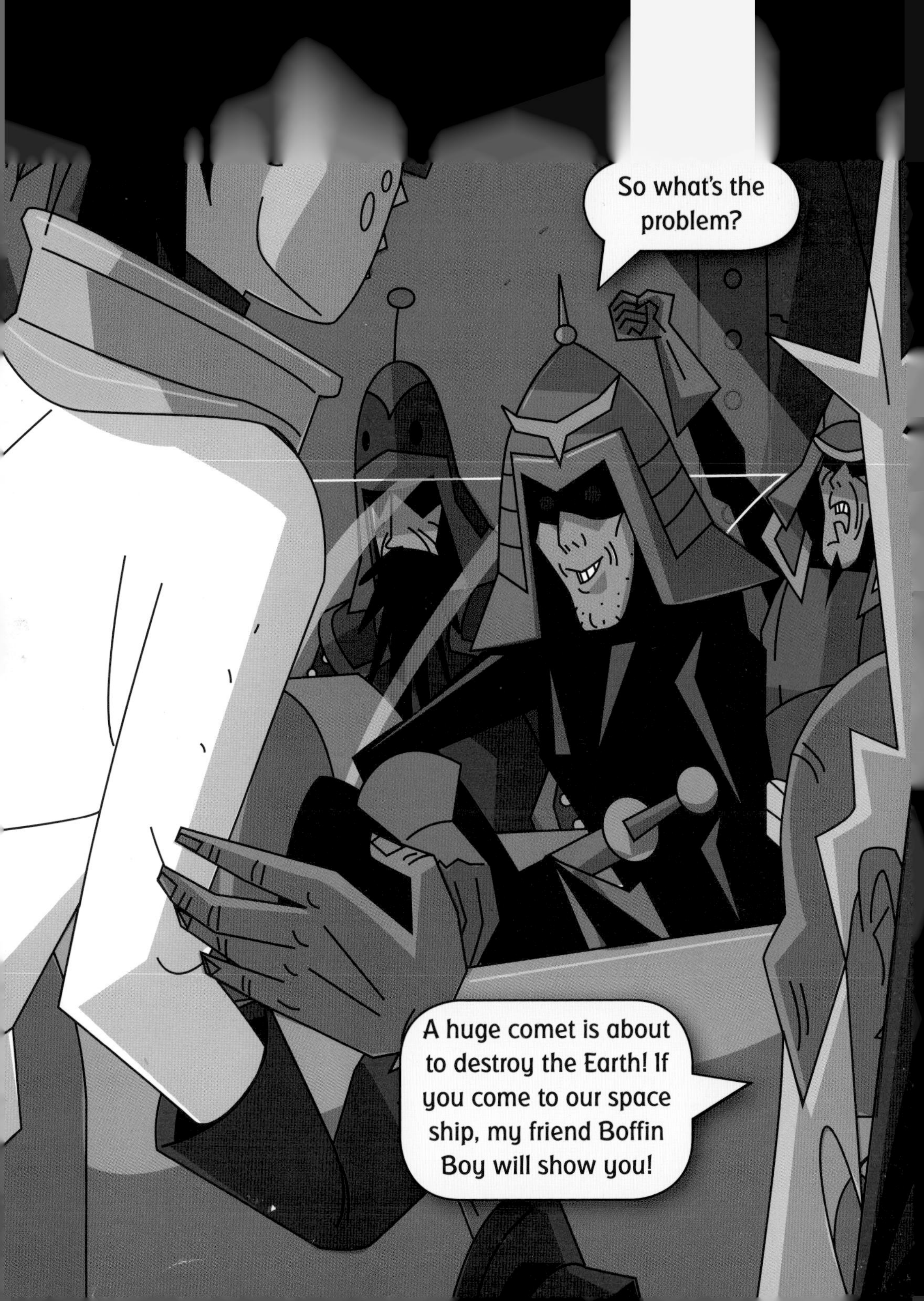
So what's the problem?
A huge comet is about to destroy the Earth! If you come to our space ship, my friend Boffin Boy will show you!

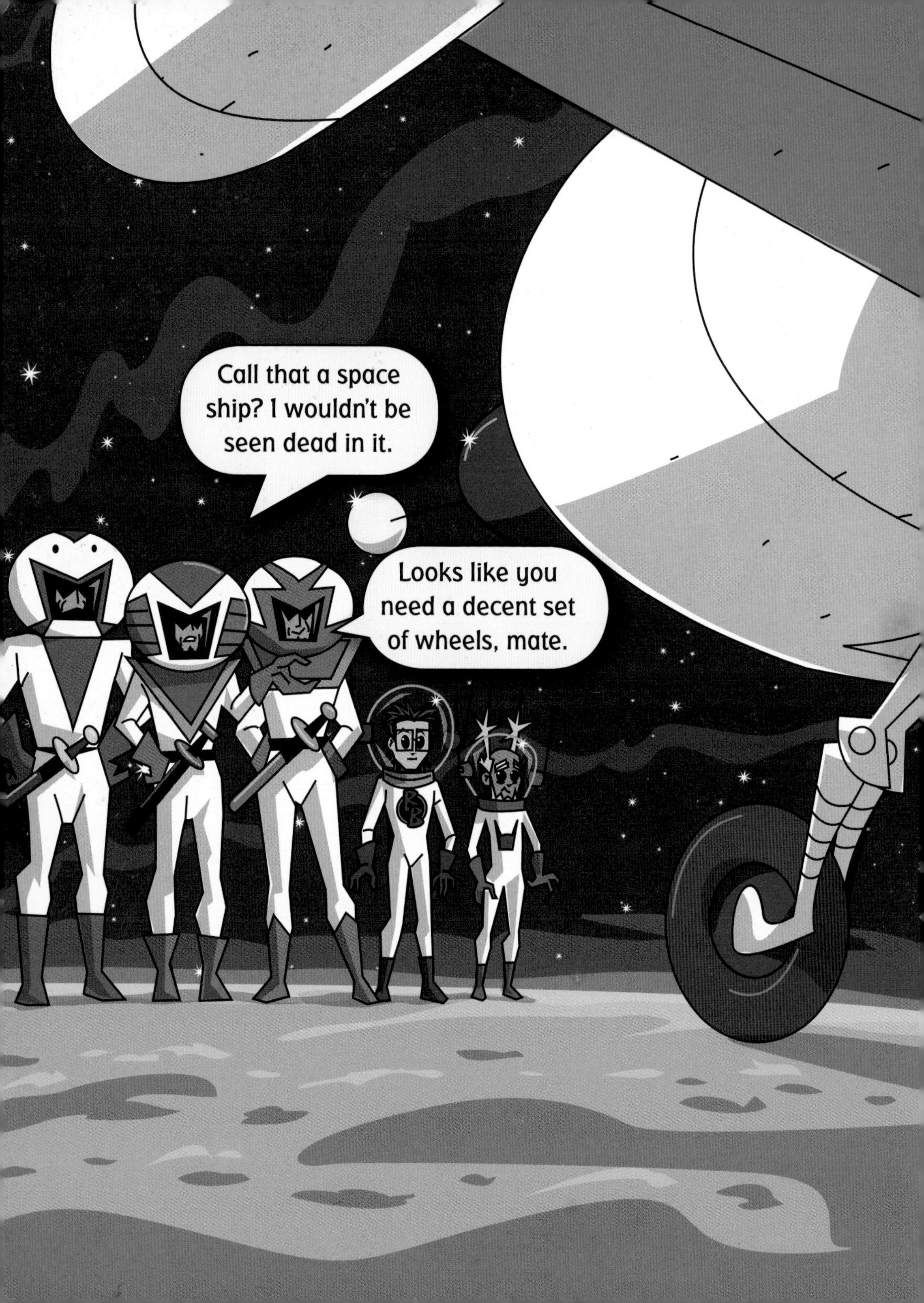
Call that a space ship? I wouldn't be seen dead in it.
Looks like you need a decent set of wheels, mate.

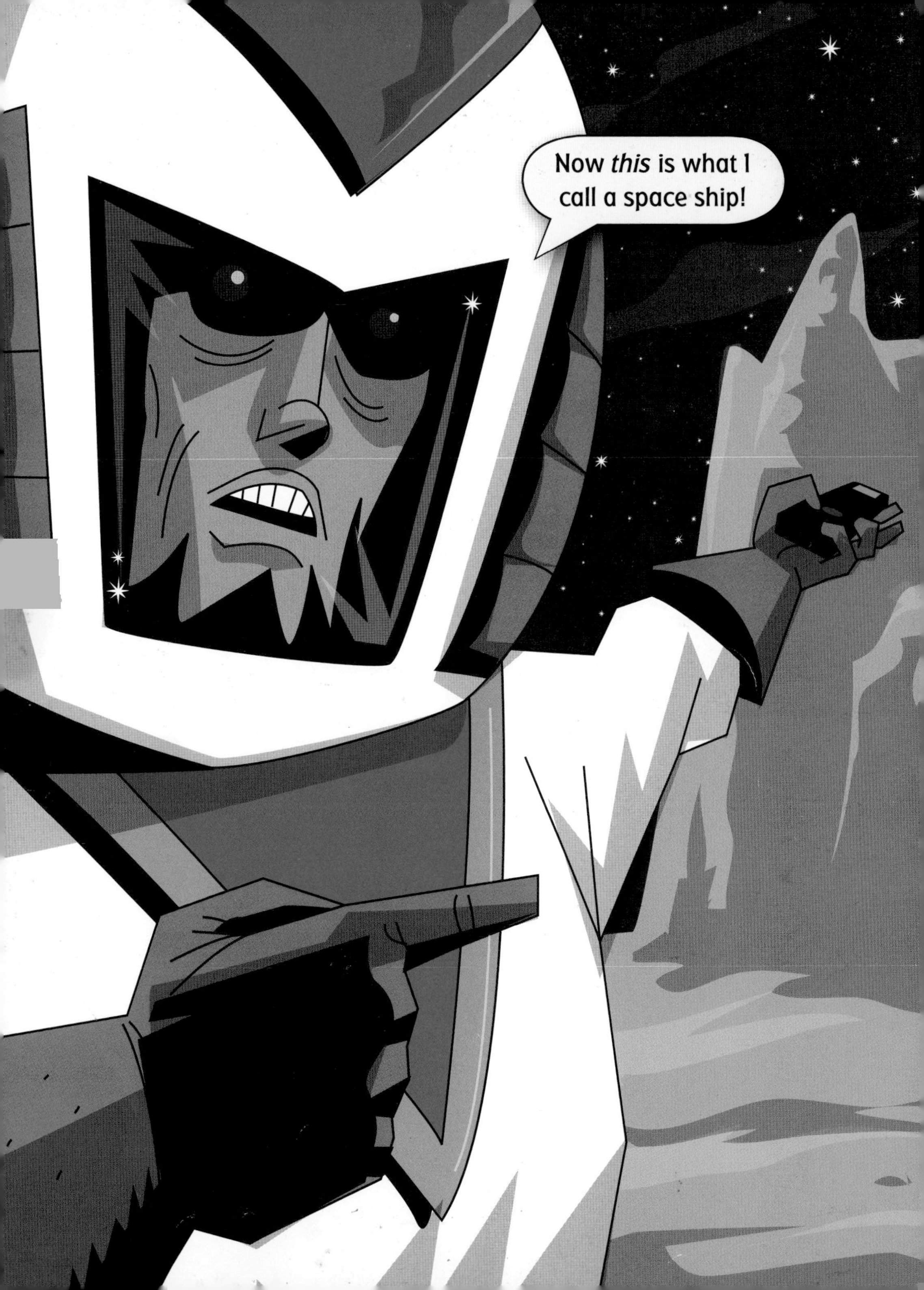
Now *this* is what I call a space ship!

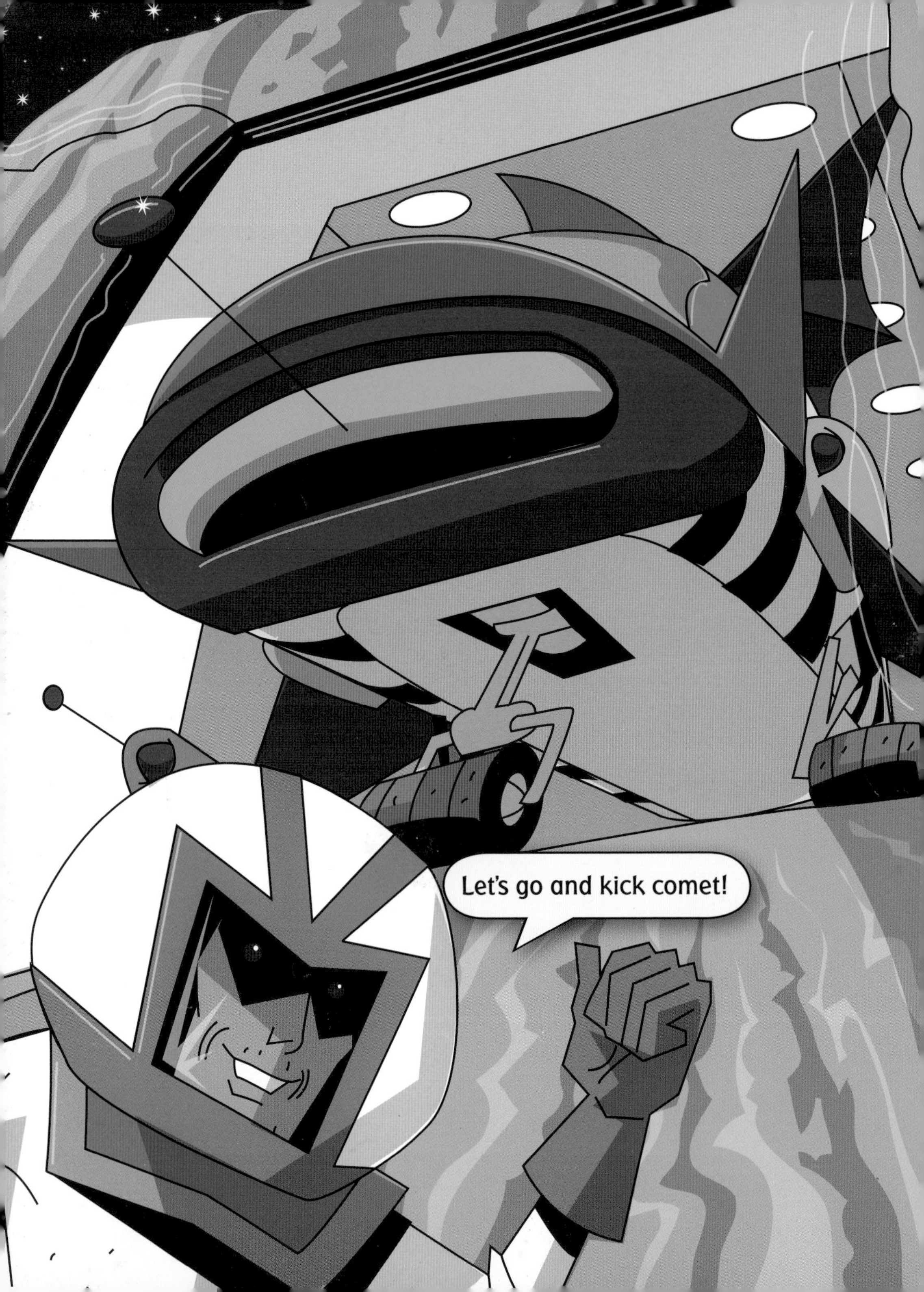
Let's go and kick comet!

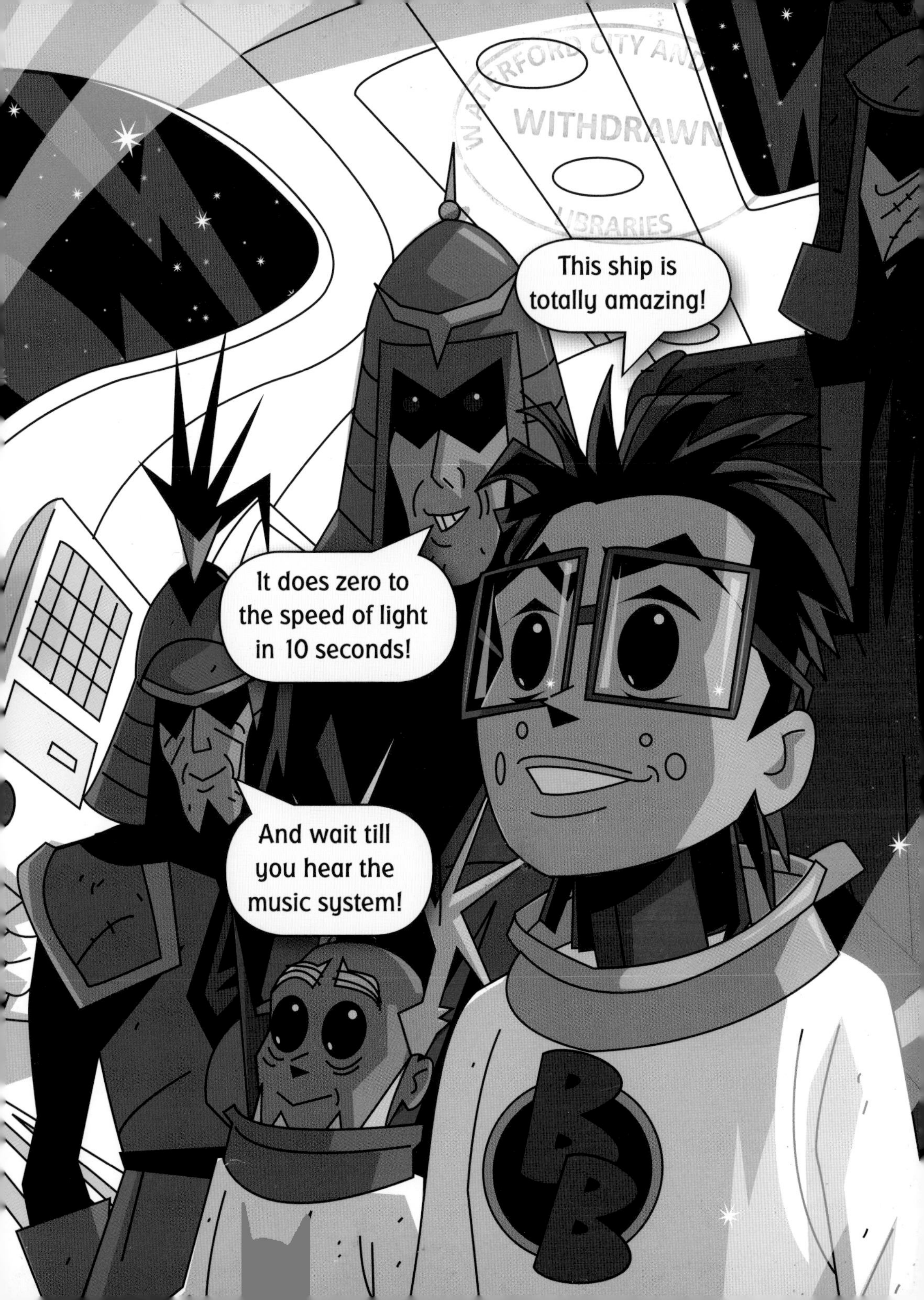
This ship is totally amazing!
It does zero to the speed of light in 10 seconds!
And wait till you hear the music system!

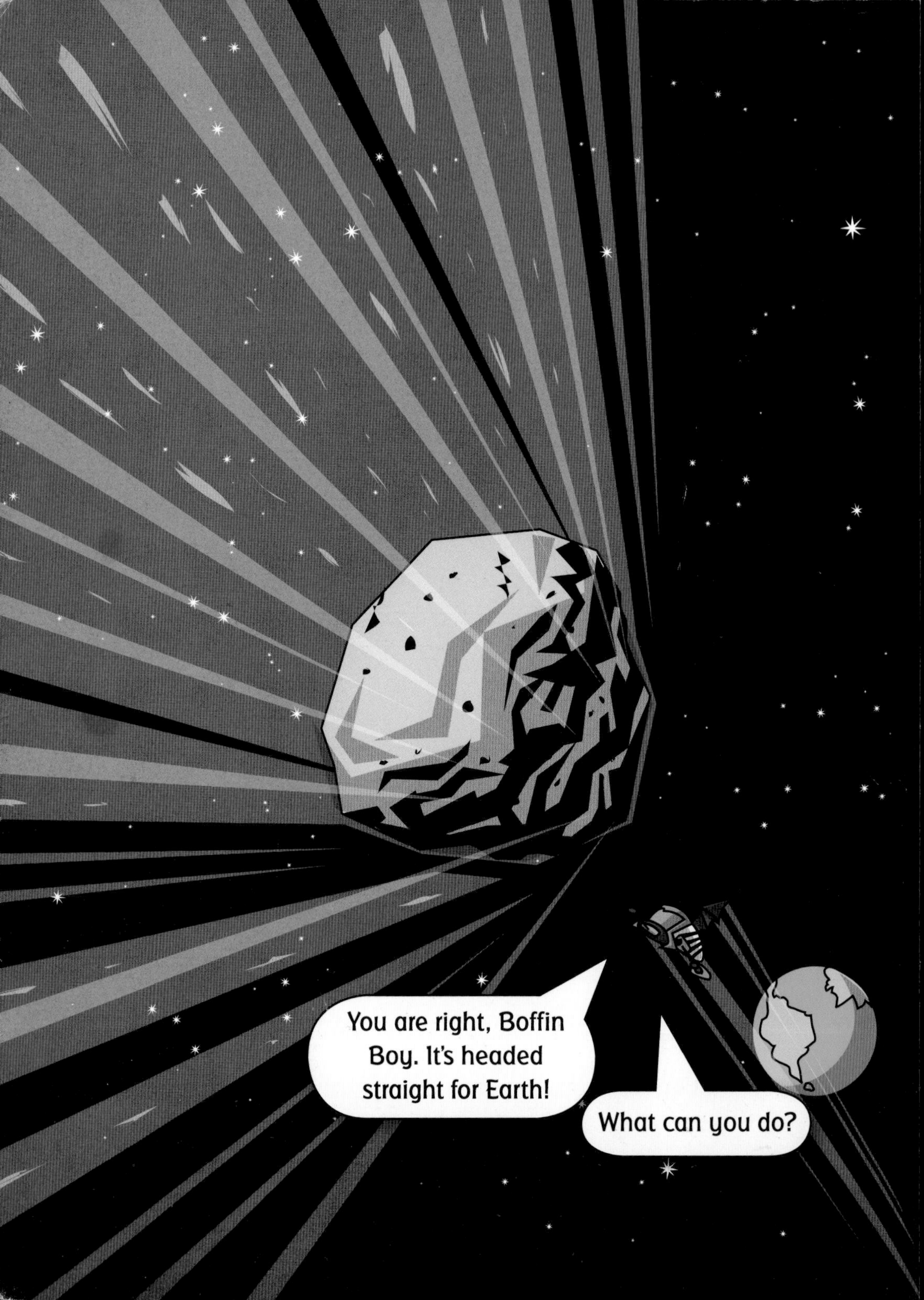
You are right, Boffin Boy. It's headed straight for Earth!
What can you do?

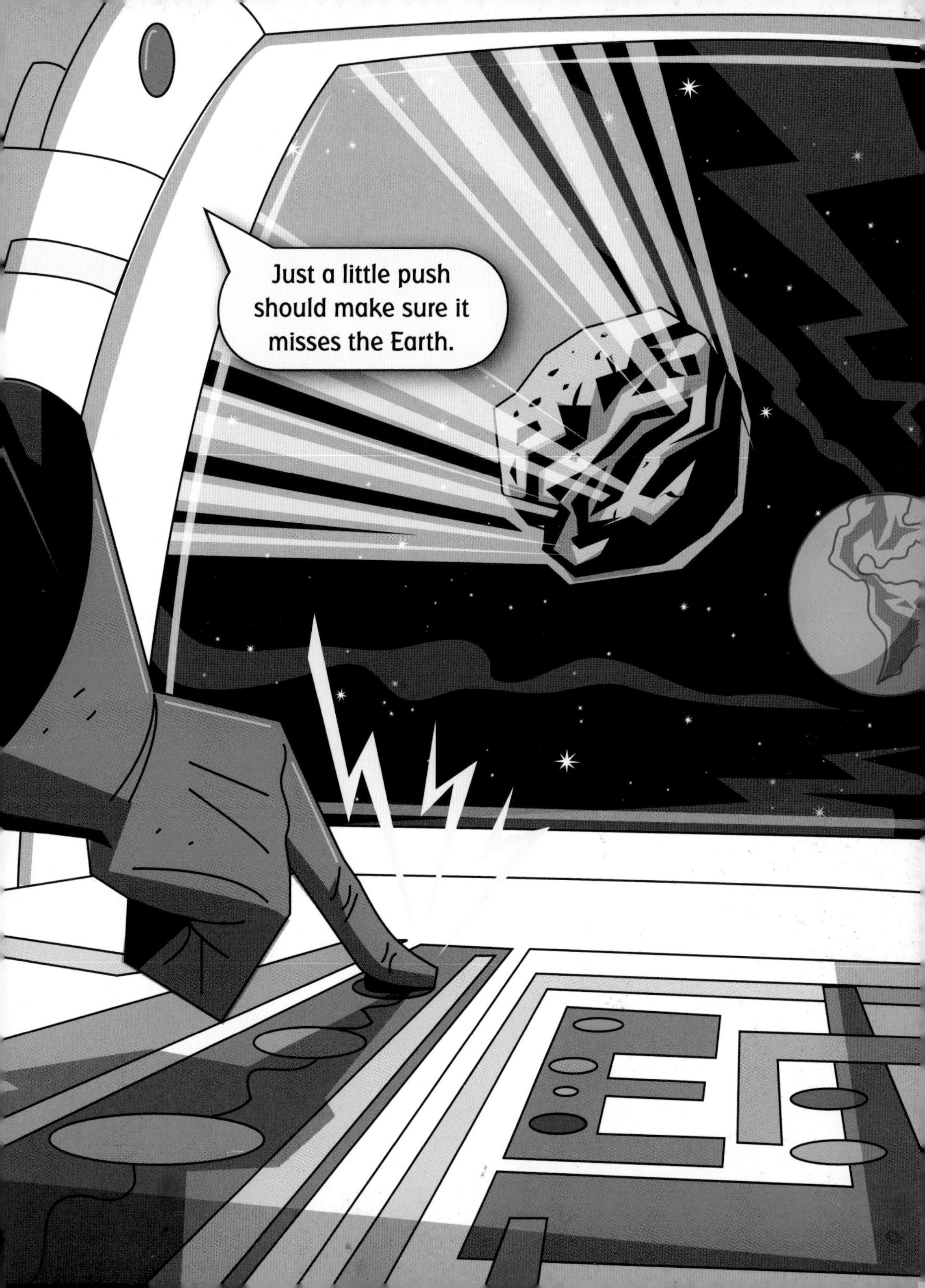
Just a little push should make sure it misses the Earth.

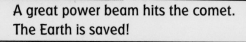

A great power beam hits the comet.
The Earth is saved!

Whoops! I should
have turned the
power down a bit!

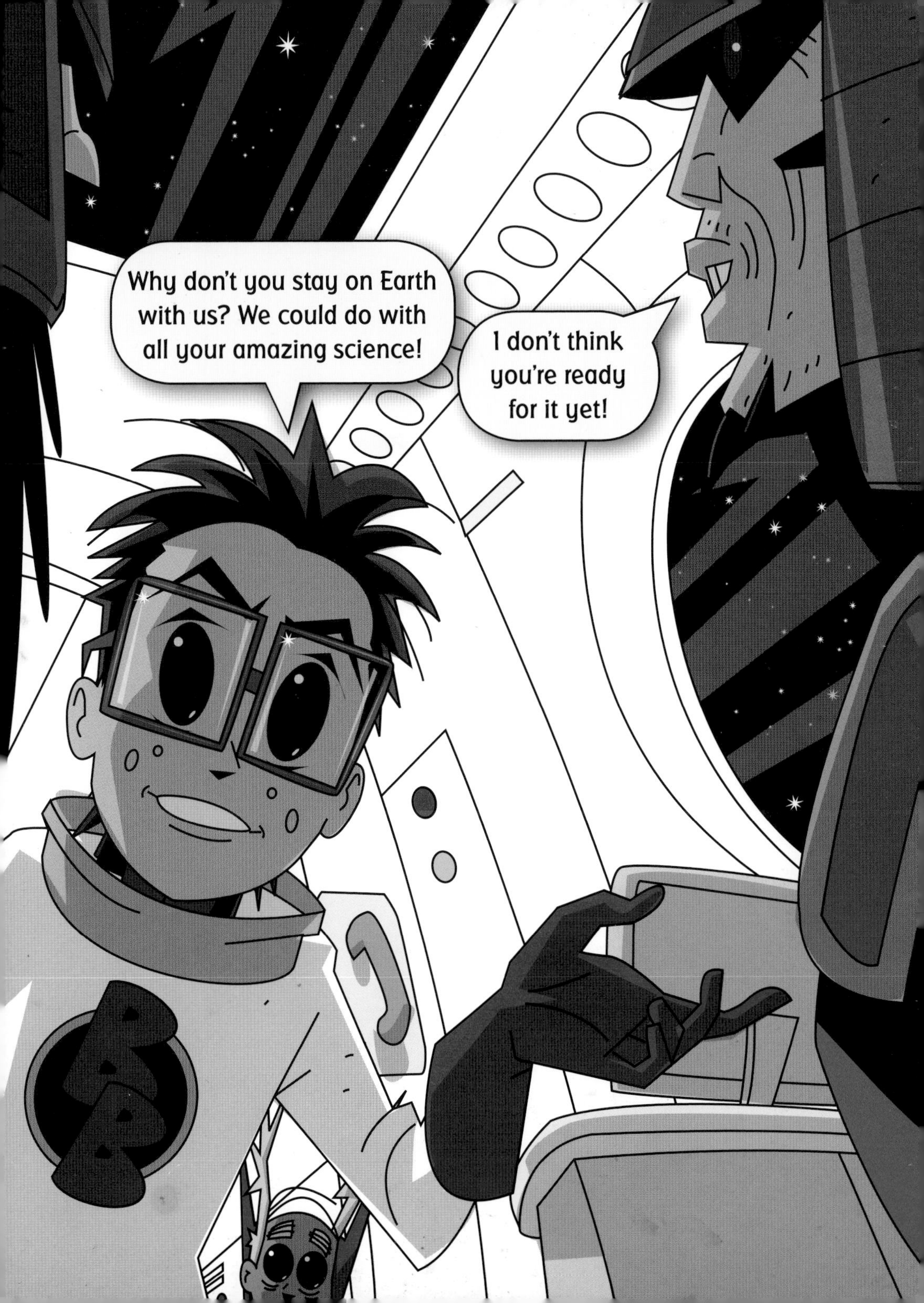
Why don't you stay on Earth with us? We could do with all your amazing science!
I don't think you're ready for it yet!

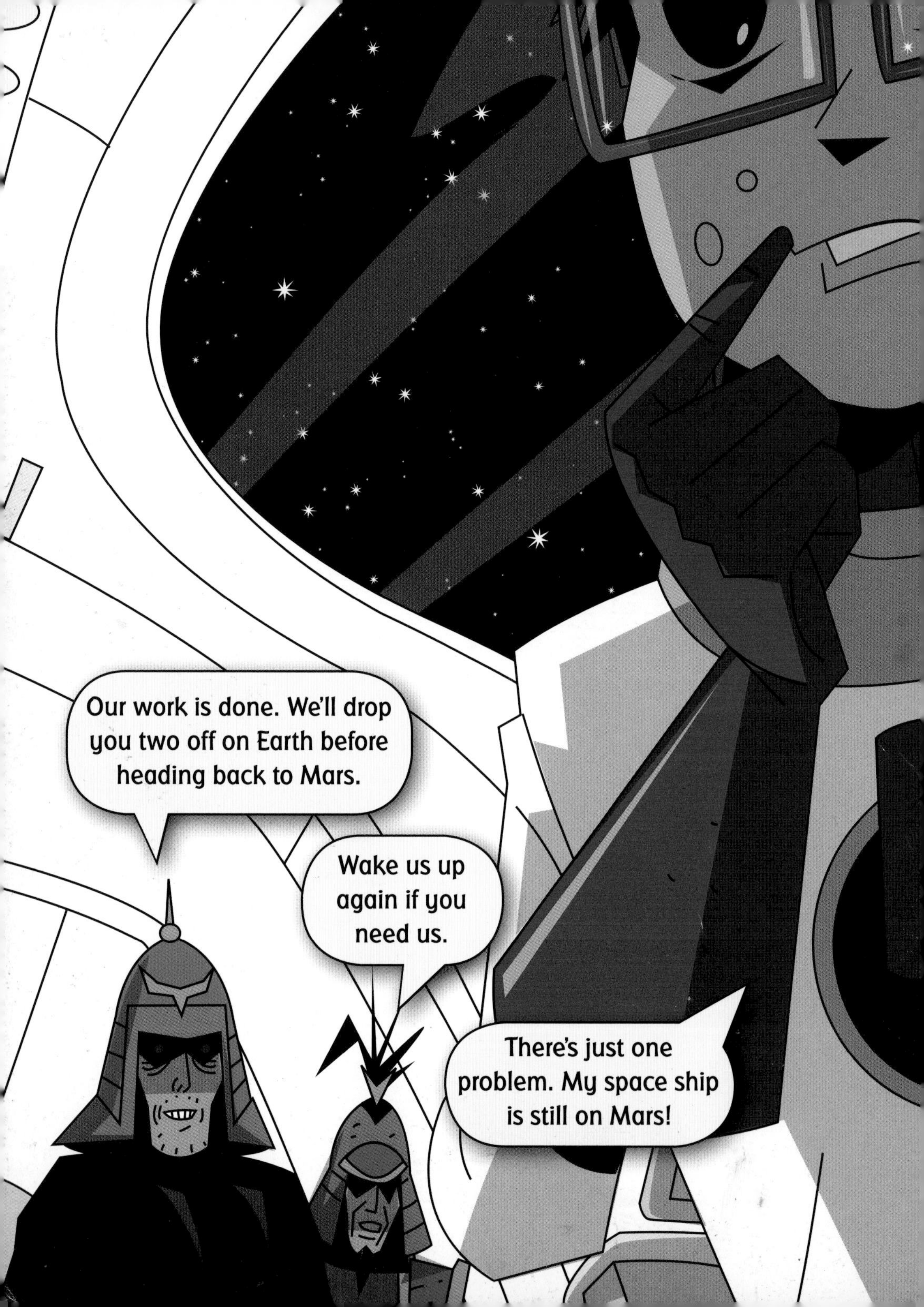

Our work is done. We'll drop you two off on Earth before heading back to Mars.
Wake us up again if you need us.
There's just one problem. My space ship is still on Mars!

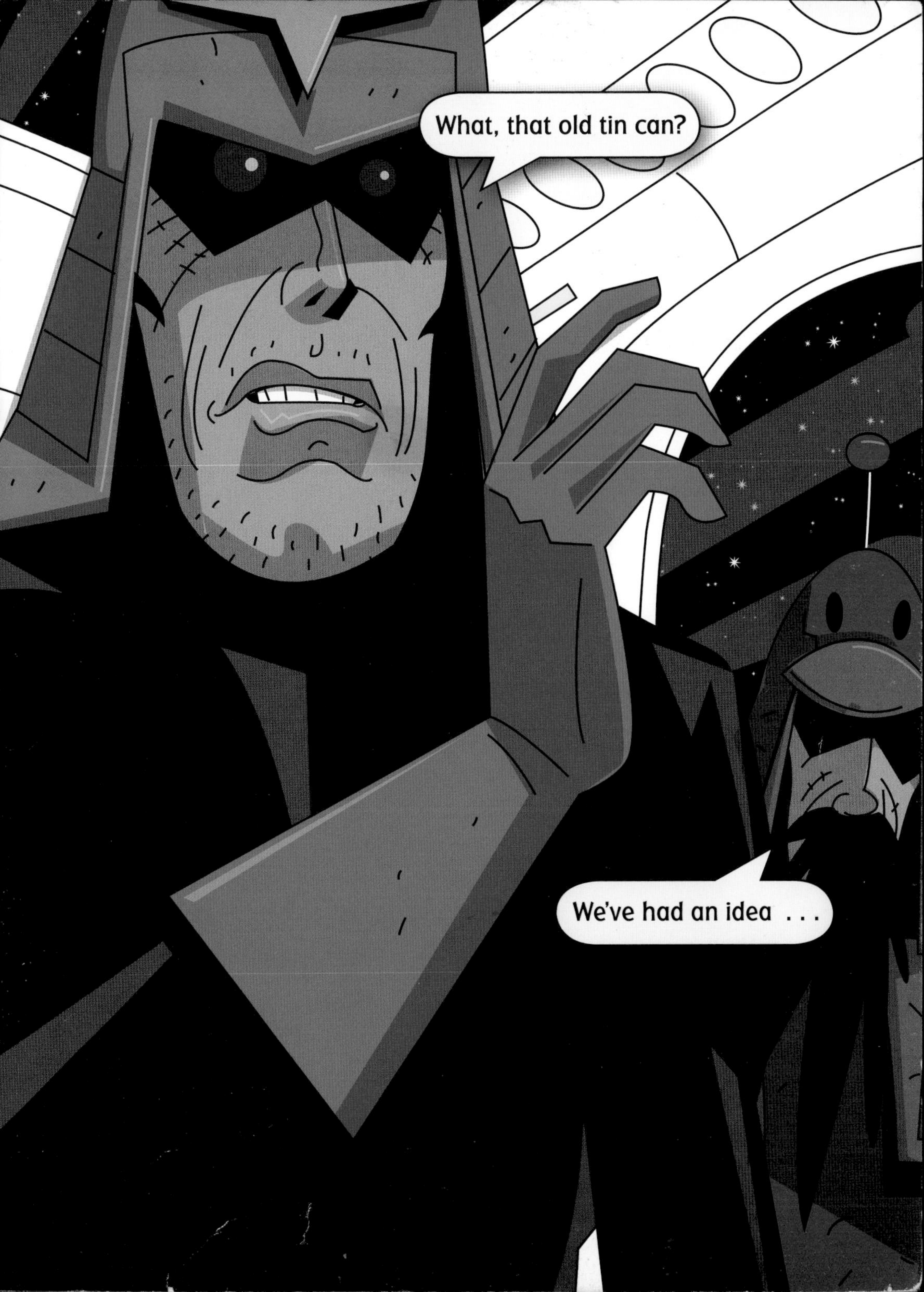
What, that old tin can?
We've had an idea . . .

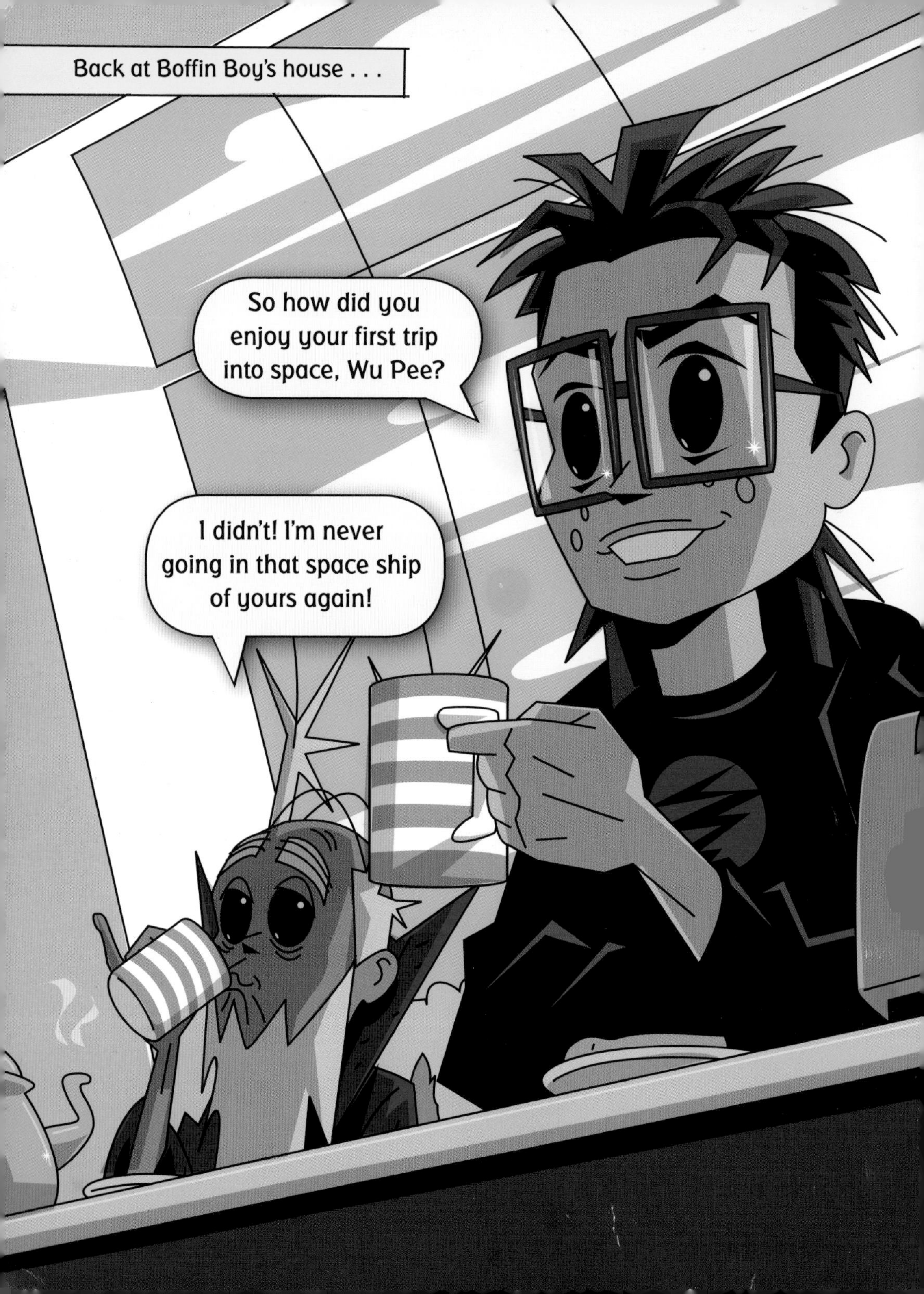
Back at Boffin Boy's house . . .
So how did you enjoy your first trip into space, Wu Pee?
I didn't! I'm never going in that space ship of yours again!

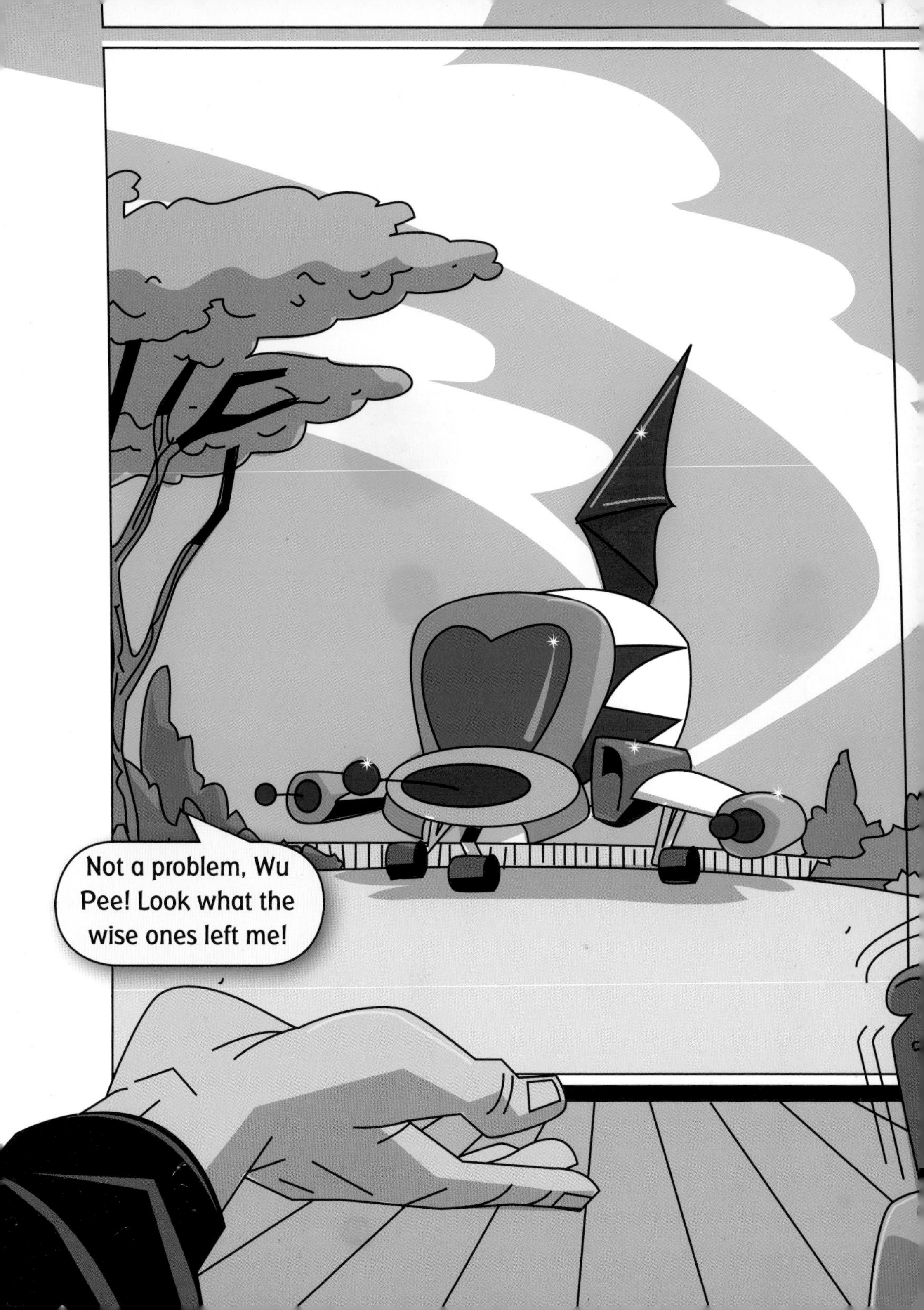
Not a problem, Wu Pee! Look what the wise ones left me!

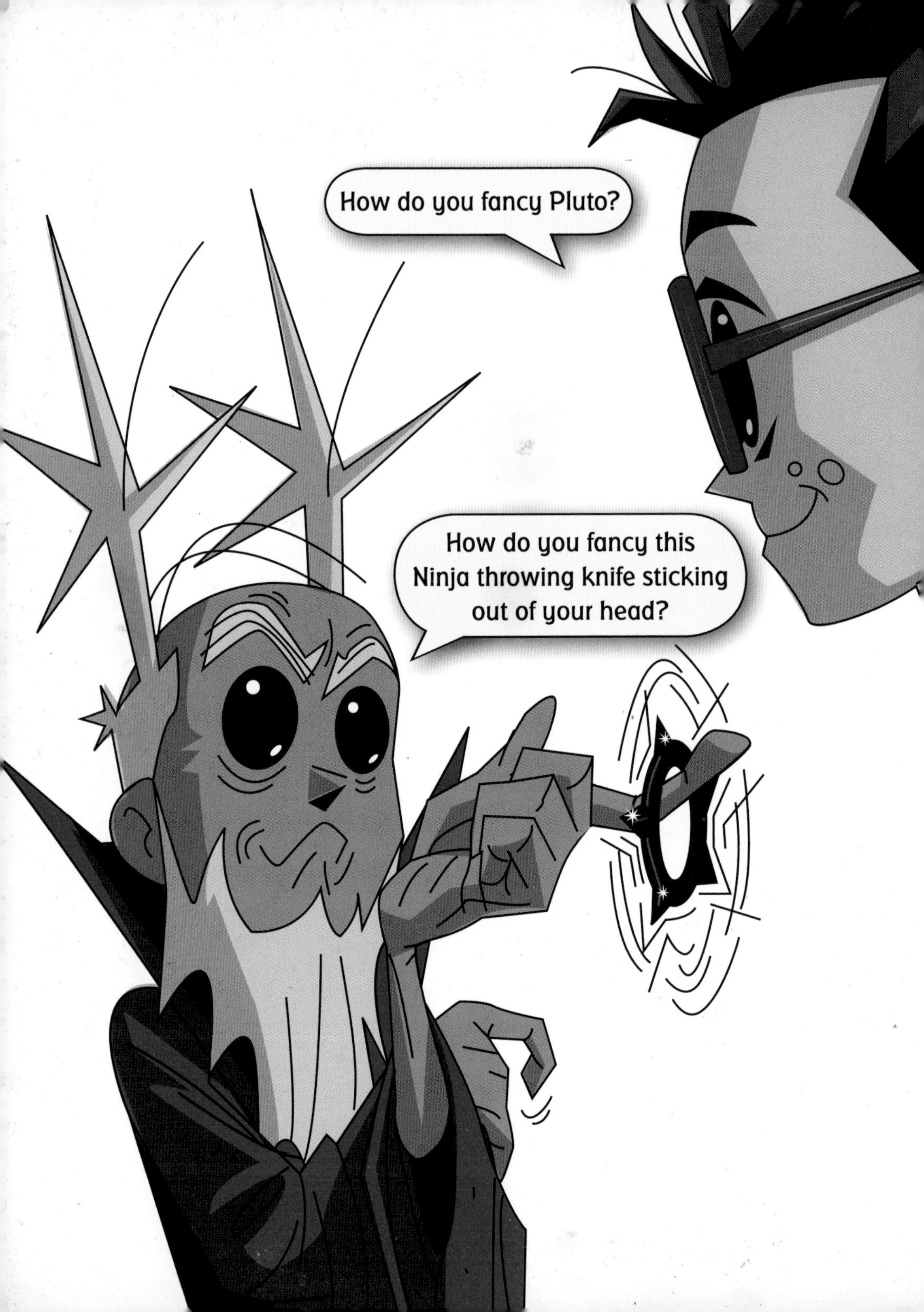
How do you fancy Pluto?
How do you fancy this Ninja throwing knife sticking out of your head?

ABOUT THE AUTHOR

David Orme has written over 200 books including poetry collections, fiction and non-fiction, and school text books. When he is not writing books he travels around the UK, giving performances, running writing workshops and courses.

Find out more at:
www.magic-nation.com.

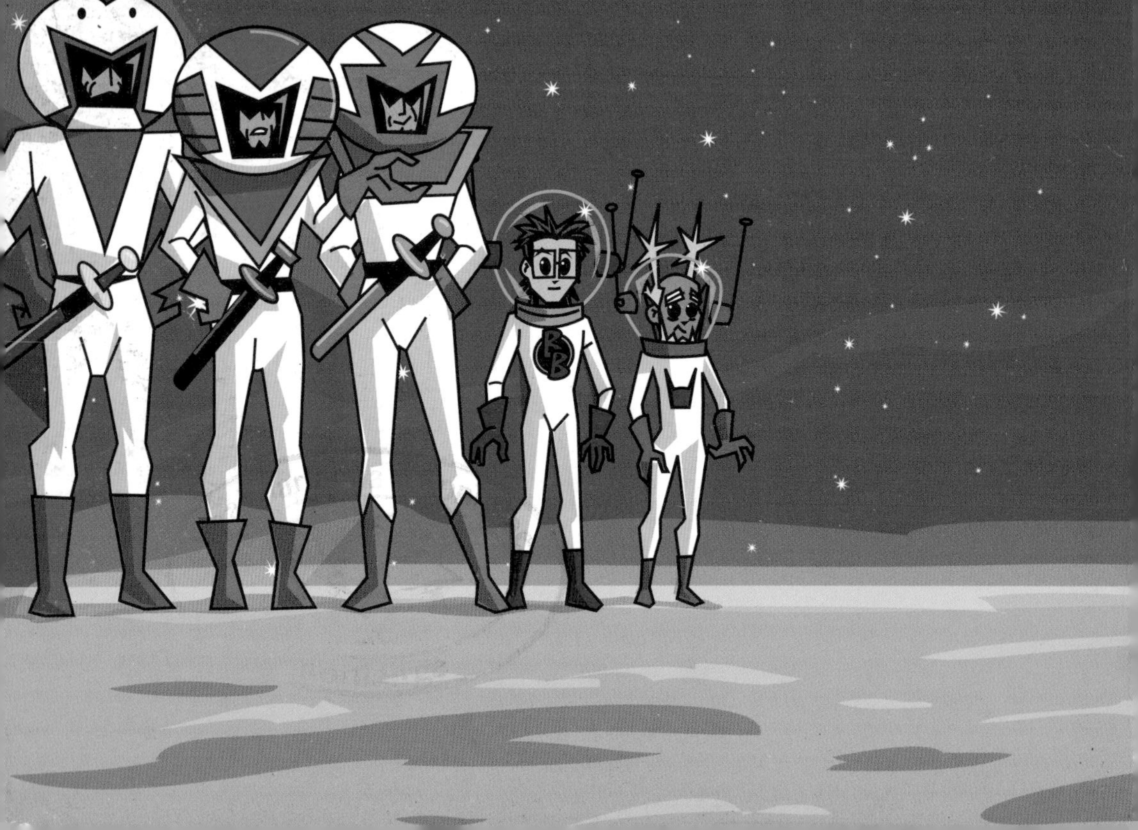